A FAMILY ALBUM

Also by the Duke of Windsor

A KING'S STORY

THE CROWN AND THE PEOPLE 1902–1953

A FAMILY ALBUM

BY

THE DUKE OF WINDSOR

CASSELL · LONDON

CASSELL & COMPANY LTD
35 Red Lion Square · London WC1
and at
MELBOURNE · SYDNEY · TORONTO
CAPE TOWN · AUCKLAND

First published in book form 1960

Set in 12 on 14pt. Garamond
and printed in Great Britain by
Cox & Wyman, Ltd., London, Fakenham and Reading
F.760

CONTENTS

LIST OF ILLUSTRATIONS

Between pages 104 and 105

Between pages 136 and 137

CHAPTER I

WINDSOR REVISITED

When, from time to time, the Duchess and I return for a few days to England from France, where we live, or from America, where we like to spend the winter, I look around me for signs of change. One of the most striking, to me, is that nowadays I can walk about London with greater freedom than I could have done in the past. In those days a loyal crowd would have been after me, footing hot on my heels. For photography, killing the private lives of princes, had made me familiar to all. But today few people recognize me, as I stroll through the streets.

After all, it is now twenty-three years since I left Great Britain, to lead the life of a private person. In the meantime, there has grown up a new generation, as yet unborn when I was King, that does not know me from Adam. And as for my own generation—well, having passed the mellow age of sixty, I look, very naturally, older, as indeed my contemporaries do themselves. So how should they know me? Not long ago, in Locke's the famous hatters of St. James's Street, I ran into a man whose face

I easily recognized, and with whom I exchanged a few words about fox-hunting days. But for the life of me I could not remember his name, and I had to ask the man in the shop who was fitting my hat.

Our visits to England do not follow any pattern. We went twice last year and not at all the year before. When we do go it is to see friends and to shop or for some particular mission as was the sad case in 1957, when I went to attend a memorial service for my friend and former equerry, Major Edward Metcalfe, in the Chapel Royal at St. James's Palace. 'Fruity' Metcalfe, as he was known to everybody, was the best man at my wedding, and had been my companion in many adventures, serious and otherwise, some of which are later recalled in this story. That year also saw twenty-six members of the first 'Exmouth' term gathered at a dinner in London, over which I presided, to celebrate the fiftieth anniversary of our joining the Royal Navy at the Royal Naval College at Osborne, in the Isle of Wight.

As I look around me on these visits to London, I notice each year that new buildings have shot up, not skyscraping yet, like the mammoth blocks of American cities, but beginning to tower above their neighbours. Because of the narrow streets, the traffic problem is maybe even worse than in Paris, and I have lived to see part of Hyde Park transformed into a car park. One also becomes aware of the great influx of Negroes in certain sections of London where, before the last war, the sight of a coloured person would have been a rarity. Finally, as an old Guardsman, I wonder at the strange anomaly of the sentries of the Buckingham Palace Detachment of the Queen's Guard, withdrawn from their familiar posts outside the Palace railings to within the forecourt, to protect them from the curious crowds, from whom it is the sentry's ostensible duty to protect the Queen!

But there had been other, more subtle changes. Royalty is no longer so remote from the people. After the First World War, the privacy which had traditionally enshrouded royalty was considerably diminished. Partly, this was due to technological developments. In my grandfather's day, every important news event was sketched by artists on the staffs of newspapers. People were interested in these drawings, but there was not the feeling of authenticity and immediacy. Royalty was not portrayed off guard. But then the news camera came in at the turn of the century and, by the end of the First World War, the development of the high-speed shutter, improved techniques of artificial lighting, and highly sensitive films made it possible to invade the privacy of all public figures to a great extent. Then radio, and finally television, brought the voices and images of royalty into every home. These new means of communication whetted the public appetite for what was termed 'human interest' and the more 'human interest' people got, the more they wanted.

Then, too, in the changed world after the war, royalty became an instrument of Imperial policy. Lloyd George, as I've written in my memoirs, was anxious for me to travel in the Commonwealth, to maintain the ties the war had established, in the face of rising pressures of Nationalism and self-interest. I met far more people than my grandfather and father did. My father shook the hands of only a limited number of people. On my trips I shook thousands of hands. In fact, while I was touring Canada, my right hand became so bruised and blackened that I finally had to use my left.

It is not that the functions of royalty have changed. But the atmosphere surrounding the British monarchy has completely changed. People are more outspoken, and nobody escapes criticism any more. The people of the British Commonwealth expect more from the monarchy in exchange for the loyalty they give it. There is nothing surprising in the fact that amidst all the changes that have taken place, after two world wars and the threat of still another, the institution of monarchy is no longer a sealed house in a storm. I think I may have helped by opening the windows and letting in a little fresh air.

There is one place, however, which changes hardly at all, and that is Windsor Castle. Here is a palace essentially English in character, because it is lived in; so much more personal in its atmosphere, for all its bulk, than the Château de Versailles and other continental palaces, for all their past glories and classical splendours. I take pleasure in the way it broods, with an air of comfortable benevolence, down over the homely town of Windsor, while to the South spreads the spacious Great Park, with the Long Walk stretching three miles through the soft green English landscape and the meadows of the Home Park to the south, refreshed by the waters of the slowly winding Thames. I naturally know the road to Windsor blindfold, from the many years I have been going there. I know where to turn, to avoid the congestion of Staines, and I know the exact spot, before Datchet, where the Castle first comes into view, rising quietly on the horizon to dream above the fields in a grey silhouette.

Hundreds of thousands of people from all parts of the

world visit Windsor Castle when the Sovereign is not in residence, strolling up the hill to the State Apartments—though hardly as in the days of George III, when the place was a free-for-all playground for the schoolchildren of Windsor. So it was when I visited Windsor last summer.

In the private apartments of the Sovereign, sumptuous with their gilded woodwork and plaster, their elaborate doors from Carlton House, their rich brocaded walls of green and crimson, my thoughts went back years. We had happy times there as children, especially in the long corridor built by George IV to accommodate some of the finest of the royal collection of pictures, and incidentally to save the walk across the courtyard, from one part of the Castle to another, which George III had to take in all weathers to visit his family. Of this corridor, as Sir Owen Morshead, the late librarian at Windsor, records, Mr. Creevey remarked: 'My eye, what a spot for a walky-talky!' We kids found it an admirable spot for more boisterous pursuits, running races and playing hide-and-seek among the marble busts.

Little had been changed in these private apartments, beyond the rehanging of some pictures and the redecoration of a room here and there. I missed, over the Gothic dining-room sideboard, a large picture by Jean-Baptiste Detaille, which I had always liked, of my grandfather and his younger brother, my great-uncle Arthur, the Duke of Connaught, riding on splendid chargers, uniformed and finely plumed, on a field day at Aldershot.

But over the fireplace in this same room still hangs Benjamin Constant's portrait of Queen Victoria, the Garter ribbon across her chest painted the wrong shade of blue. There is a story that the Order and ribbon were sent to the artist at his studio in Paris, with a request that he should darken the colour. On opening the parcel, he exclaimed in delighted astonishment: 'The Order of the Garter for me! What an honour!' On learning that the Order was only a loan, he took offence, so it is said, and refused to repaint it.

But the Garter ribbon across the chest of my father, in his portrait by Sir Oswald Birley in another room, shines forth in its true blue colour. I always admired this portrait, but my father did not care for it. The painting of the hands did not please him, so he hung it behind a door, where few could see it. One of the first things I did, on ascending the Throne, was to move it to a position of prominence. And there, I was glad to see, it still remains.

The portrait that Sir Arthur Cope painted of me in Garter dress had been removed, I learnt, to Buckingham Palace. Very few portraits of me, painted from life, exist—doubtless because I am too restless to make a good sitter. I was painted by Sir William Orpen, for the Royal and Ancient Golf Club at St. Andrews, of which I was once Captain. This was one of Orpen's last portraits before he died. Unfortunately, he never painted my father, and for a special reason. Orpen was a convivial man, who liked always to have a glass of whisky beside him, and to replenish it at intervals, to inspire him as he worked; and he liked the people he was painting to drink with him. My father, always the soul of courtesy, would have felt obliged to drink himself, to keep the painter company; and this he flatly refused to do.

James Gunn has painted a small portrait of me, in my Prince of Wales's robes, with the Garter, and this now hangs in the drawing-room of our house in Paris, matching a portrait of my mother by Sir William Llewellyn. Sargent once did a sketch of me; so did Flamenq, when I was studying in France, and later, when I came to live there, another French painter, Drian. His sketch now hangs in the dining-room of our Mill in the country, near Paris—appropriately enough, since we bought the place from Drian himself. Otherwise, as far as the painter's brush is concerned, my true features will not unduly inflict posterity, which will be little the worse for that.

Wandering through the rooms and the corridors of Windsor, I opened a door and found myself in a dust-sheeted room. This was the room in which I made my Abdication broadcast in 1936. There in the window was the chair in which I sat on that occasion, and the desk on which I placed my script. Outside the window the green English landscape spread away to the horizon, with hardly a house, far less a gasworks or a factory chimney, to mar its gentle rural outlines. Looking out at the view and reflecting on that historic occasion, I found I had no twinge of regret, leading, as the Duchess and I have since done, a very happy and contented private life.

Later I walked across to the Library, which was William IV's contribution to the Castle. Here again childhood memories came surging back. Here was the tall library ladder on which, as kids, we used to wheel one another, with shrieks of joy, up and down the austere Gothic corridors lined with bookshelves.

Near by I recognized a large case full of miniatures which have always interested me. They portray a number of officers of the 10th Light Dragoons, now the 10th Hussars, picturesque in their busbies and plumes. In the centre is their Colonel-in-Chief, George, Prince of Wales, afterwards the Prince Regent and George IV. The regiment was usually stationed at Brighton, where he spent much of his time. I always heard that, at one stage in the Peninsular War, when 'Prinny' refused to allow it to go to the front, many of the officers insisted on going, getting themselves posted to other units. One who did not go was Beau Brummell, of whom I shall have more to say in these pages. This dandyish officer, who had little taste for wars and other such uncomfortable pursuits, resigned his commission on hearing that the regiment was due to be posted from Brighton so far afield as Manchester.

But one of my favourite haunts in the domains of Windsor Castle is Frogmore, a little-known Georgian house with a long Regency portico, only a few minutes' walk down the hill. Of this house, where my father and mother lived as Prince and Princess of Wales, I have childhood memories. My father's favourite recreation was shooting, or what I used to call 'banging', which occupied his leisure for six months of the year. But my mother, tired of shooting parties and anxious to evade those to which my father was invited, would bring us kids here to Frogmore each year, while my father 'banged' relentlessly away in the north.

I now rang the doorbell, to be answered by Bertha, for long the house's faithful caretaker. During the fifteen years which elapsed between the Duchess's and my marriage and our final acquisition of a home of our own in France, our furniture and silver and other possessions were stored at Frogmore in Bertha's charge, and she still takes care of my old uniforms, conscientiously laid away

The neck-high lace collars worn (*above*) by Charles I in the triple portrait by Van Dyck and (*below*) by Charles II in the portrait by Janssens of him dancing at The Hague, were to be supplanted by the cravat

In this portrait of George III by Gainsborough, the King is wearing one of the forerunners of the morning-coat as a part of his Windsor Uniform

Lord Byron proclaimed a reaction against 'Brummellism' by wearing the loose open collars and flowing cravat that are shown in the portrait of him by Sandars

Queen Victoria's railway saloon, which was always lit by oil and candle lamps

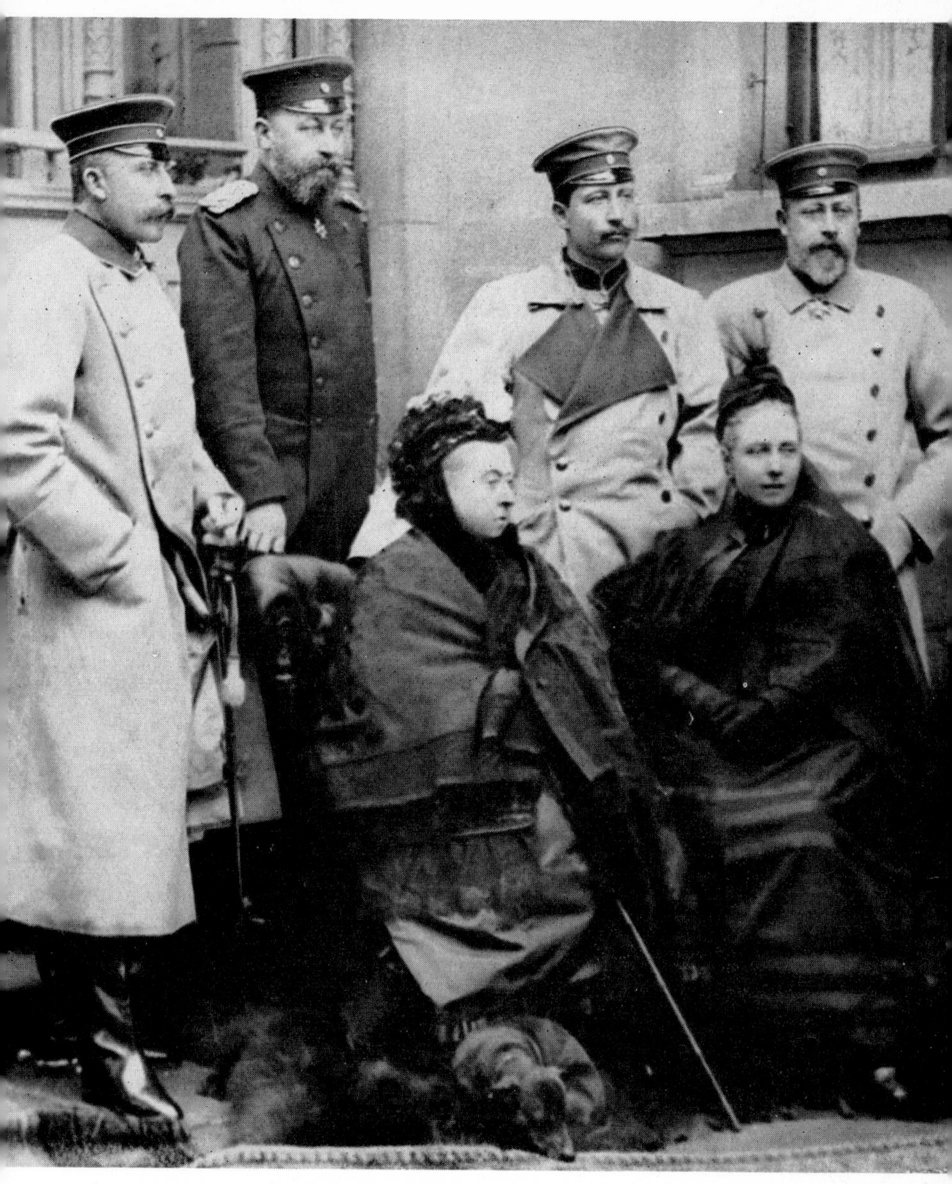

Queen Victoria is seated with her daughter, the Dowager Empress of Germany. Behind them (*from right to left*) are standing King Edward VII, then Prince of Wales, the Kaiser, and the Dukes of Edinburgh and Connaught

(*Left*) After the Prince Consort's death, which took place a few months after this picture of him with Queen Victoria was taken, the kind of fancy waistcoat which he is wearing went out of fashion for eighty years

Benjamin Constant's portrait of Queen Victoria hangs over the fireplace in the dining-room in the Sovereign's private apartments at Windsor, with the Garter ribbon painted the wrong shade of blue

Edward VII, then Prince of Wales, with Prince Alfred on the Isle of Wight in 1855. The floppy hats, loose collars and ties and open jackets contrast with the stiffer children's wear of the later Victorian era

A semi-formal portrait of Edward VII at the age of twelve, in an almost open 'Byron' collar and loose neckwear

Edward VII at the age of fifteen, wearing the Windsor Uniform, for his confirmation

in mothballs. Frogmore—a house, incidentally, with only one bathroom, installed on the ground floor by my father—has become a kind of museum of unwanted royal possessions, including my mother's own unusual collection of Victoriana—souvenirs of royal weddings, papier-mâché objects, domed waxed fruits and flowers—which she had amassed throughout the years.

Frogmore has a romantic garden, well laid out, with undulating lawns and a winding lake, lush with water-lilies, shaded by spreading cedars and weeping willows. Rhododendrons grow in profusion and, even if some of the Ponticum species might be weeded out, the general effect is one of peaceful beauty, far removed from the noisy world outside.

In my childhood, however, untroubled still by such fastidious horticultural tastes, my brothers and sister and I would career along the well-kept paths on our bicycles, free-wheeling and pedalling around the imposing Rotunda erected, in the classical style, as a memorial to my great-great-grandmother, the Duchess of Kent, whose daughter, Queen Victoria, is buried, with the Prince Consort in the Mausoleum near by. Queen Victoria used to come to this garden on fine mornings to eat her breakfast with her relations in a small red-brick pavilion. My mother liked to come here, too, drinking tea in the afternoon underneath the big tree on the lawn and working on a needle-point rug.

I too depend on my cup of tea, as most self-respecting Britons do. Whenever I am travelling in such arid, tealess lands as France and America, I carry a tartan zip-bag containing Thermoses filled with this delectable beverage. Having brought it with me in the car from London, I now sat on a garden bench, this warm July afternoon, and poured the tea out into a plastic cup. Under its soothing influence I relaxed and reflected on the day I had spent at Windsor Castle.

The place itself had changed little enough, I thought, since the days when George III made it habitable and George IV embellished it, displaying a mastery of the arts unrivalled by any subsequent member of my family. The institution and conception of the monarchy are unchanging. But the life lived within the Castle and its precincts, by monarchs throughout the centuries, had changed a great deal. You had only to look at those family portraits to see how, for example, the dress of royalty had changed. And their manners and customs, their social behaviour, their recreations, their tastes in eating and drinking, their means of locomotion had changed drastically as well.

I reflected that my own life, covering a span of years between the reign of Queen Victoria and that of Elizabeth II, has had its share of changes that might be worthy of record. And so this short book was born.

CHAPTER II

CLOTHES AND THE PRINCE

There survives a letter written in 1851 by Queen Victoria to her eldest son, the Prince of Wales, my grandfather-to-be but then a boy of ten years old. It appears from this letter—drafted, I rather suspect, by the Prince Consort, but underlined, in characteristic fashion, by the Queen—that my grandfather, at this early age, already enjoyed financial independence, a degree of emancipation which I myself was not to achieve until the more advanced age of fifteen, following his death, my father's Accession to the Throne, and my own succession to the revenues of the Duchy of Cornwall. It was then his own responsibility to order his meals 'in accordance with what the physicians say is good for you'. From now onwards he was to order his own clothes as well.

'Dress,' his mother writes to him, 'is a trifling matter which might not be raised to too much importance in our own eyes. But it gives also the one outward sign from which people in general can and often do judge upon the *inward* state of mind and feeling of a person; for this they all see, while the other they cannot see. On that account it is of some importance particularly in persons of high rank. I must now say that we do not wish to control your own tastes and fancies which, on the contrary, we wish you to indulge and develop, but we do *expect* that you will never wear anything *extravagant* or *slang*, not because we don't like it but because it would prove a want of self-respect and be an offence against decency, leading, as it has often done before in others, to an indifference to what is morally wrong.'

In other words, clothes make the prince—at least in the eyes of the people. So early an introduction to the art—to say nothing of the morality—of costume must certainly have contributed to my grandfather's emergence in later life as the best-dressed of princes, in this respect rivalling, but in no way imitating, his dandyish predecessor, King George IV. Such a principle used sometimes to tempt me to wonder, when I myself emerged from childhood to a relative maturity, whether in the eyes of certain sections of the Press I was not more of a glorified clothes-peg than the heir-apparent. Nevertheless, my great-grandmother's homily expresses sentiments with which I cordially agree and have endeavoured, in my own modest way, to put into practice.

In this context, let it not be assumed that clothes have ever been a fetish of mine. Rather have I become, by force of circumstances and upbringing, clothes-conscious. My position as Prince of Wales dictated that I should always be well and suitably dressed for every conceivable occasion. And how varied those occasions have been!

The same, of course, was true of my father. Now that I come to think of it, clothes were always a favourite topic of his conversation. With my father, it was not so much a discussion as to who he considered to be well or badly dressed; it was more usually a diatribe against anyone who dressed differently from himself. Those who did he called 'cads'. Unfortunately the 'cads' were the majority of my generation, by the time I grew up, and I was, of course, one of them. Being my father's eldest son, I bore the brunt of his criticism.

Meanwhile, the Prince Consort was to enlarge on Queen Victoria's precepts in a paper of instruction 'for the guidance of gentlemen appointed to attend on the Prince of Wales'. It refers to the qualities which distinguish a gentleman in society, with especial regard to his manners and costume: 'The appearance, deportment and dress of a gentleman consist perhaps more in the absence of certain offences against good taste, and in careful avoidance of vulgarities and exaggerations of any kind, however generally they may be the fashion of the day, than in the adherence to any rules which can be exactly laid down. A gentleman does not indulge in careless, self-indulgent, lounging ways, such as lolling in armchairs, or on sofas, slouching in his gait, or placing himself in unbecoming attitudes, with his hands in his pockets, or in any position in which he appears to consult more the idle ease of the moment than the maintenance of the decorum which is characteristic of a polished gentleman. In dress, with scrupulous attention to neatness and good taste, he will never give in to the unfortunately loose and slang style which predominates at the present day. He will borrow nothing from the fashions of the groom or the gamekeeper, and whilst avoiding the frivolity and foolish vanity of dandyism, will take care that his clothes are of the best quality, well-made, and suitable to his rank and position. . . .

'To all these particulars the Prince of Wales must necessarily pay more attention than anyone else. His deportment will be more watched, his dress more criticized. There are many habits and practices and much in dress which might be quite natural and unobjectionable for these gentlemen at their own homes and in their ordinary life, which would form dangerous examples for the Prince of Wales to copy, and Her Majesty and His Royal Highness would wish them in all their habits to have regard to these consequences, and without any formality or stiffness of manner, to remember both in deportment and in dress that they are in attendance on the eldest son of the Queen.' Beau Brummell himself, a man otherwise unlikely to have found much in common with my great-grandfather, could hardly have expressed his own philosophy of clothes more aptly—though he might well have expressed it more wittily. Was it not he that laid down, for the gentlemen of his time, the principle of simplicity and restraint in costume? 'If John Bull turns to look after you,' he remarked, 'you are not well-dressed but either too stiff, too tight or too fashionable.' Sir Max Beerbohm has written of him: 'Is it not to his fine scorn of accessories that we may trace the first aim of modern dandyism, the production of the supreme effect through means the least extravagant?' This was a principle in direct contradiction to the more flamboyant male fashions of earlier generations.

These old family portraits, at Windsor and elsewhere, display, quite apart from their artistic and historical qualities, a parade of fashion through the centuries. They show, I am gratified to observe, that the Kings of England and their relatives were, on the whole, well enough dressed. They show also how gradual are the changes in men's fashions, in comparison with those of the opposite sex. From the beginning of the nineteenth century until the outbreak of the First World War, male dress changed relatively little except in cut and length and matters of detail, and by examining the portraits and photographs of my ancestors and predecessors I can trace, easily enough, the evolution of most of the garments worn today.

Charles II, for example, wears a type of frock-coat, a garment introduced in his time from Persia, which replaced the doublet and cloak. Full-skirted though it be, and bedecked with frills and flounces and furbelows, it is nevertheless recognizably the ancestor of the sterner and straighter frock-coat, worn all the world over, as formal or business dress, during the nineteenth and early twentieth centuries.

Personally, I always disliked the frock-coat, preferring the morning-coat if I had to go formal, and of this the ancestry is clearly visible in the portraits of George III. Beechey portrays him in a frock-coat, its front skirts buttoned back according to the habit of the time, to make it more comfortable for riding. From this the practice evolved of cutting the skirts to slope away, and so the morning-coat was born. In one of his portraits by Gainsborough, the King wears a coat of this kind, still differing, however, from its progeny of the following century in that it is generously be-frogged with gold braid and cut to button high at the neck, with a high-buttoning waistcoat that stretches down almost as low as the knees.

Until the middle of the eighteenth century, the elaborate costumes worn by the nobility and gentry of Great Britain were, with regard to colour and embroidery, left very much to the taste and discretion of those who could afford them. George III it was who first devised the idea of a standard dress for his family and immediate entourage, on the analogy of the liveries worn by servants. He introduced the 'Windsor uniform', and it is this that he is wearing in his portraits by both Beechey and Gainsborough.

The Windsor uniform is not a uniform in the military sense, but a dark blue tail-coat with red collar and cuffs. Essentially simple in character, it marked a contrast to the extravagant costumes of earlier periods, and was appropriate to the greater severity of the later Hanoverians. Sir Owen Morshead, the former librarian at Windsor Castle, who has made a study of the Windsor uniform, recalls that Charles II had similarly tried to introduce a standard dress for men, a century earlier. But it was killed by French ridicule, when Louis XIV put all his servants into an identical livery. George III may well have got the idea of his Windsor uniform from his cousin, Frederick the Great of Prussia, whose courtiers were similarly clothed. He was also, it seems, inspired by his admiration for Lady Pembroke, and for the dark blue livery, with red collar and cuffs, of the servants at Wilton —a livery which Lord Pembroke, on its adoption by his sovereign, tactfully changed for another.

In its undress form, the Windsor coat was also a hunt-coat. There are paintings of the King, hunting with the Buck Hounds in the Great Park, dressed in this blue coat with red collar and cuffs. It was adapted for evening wear, in the same way as the red tail-coats worn by members of the different hunts in Britain, America and other countries today.

Though designed primarily for wear at Windsor, after George III had made the Castle his home, the uniform was sometimes worn elsewhere. Once at Kew, during the King's insanity, he was heard to remark, during a lucid moment, that it was nice to see everyone wearing Windsor uniform. It made him feel at home, 'the place I like best in the world'. George IV wore the uniform at Brighton, but his brother, William IV, discontinued it altogether.

Then Queen Victoria revived it for her family, her household and a few favoured persons. I can remember it being worn on formal occasions at Windsor, in the day-time. The Queen's equerries, meeting distinguished guests at Windsor Station, used to wear it with dark, or even pepper-and-salt, trousers and top hat. But after the First World War my father confined its use to evening wear, with knee-breeches. Now I understand that even these have been discarded in favour of trousers.

The Windsor uniform, adapting itself to the sartorial changes of its time, may be regarded as a prototype of the more formal male fashions of two generations. In the nineteenth-century portraits, the 'frogs' have disappeared from the coat, giving place to gilt buttons; the neck-line is lowered, by means of longer lapels; the coat is cut away, and the waistcoat has risen from the knee to the waistline, where it more properly belongs. In the Long Gallery at Windsor, the Duke of Wellington, as painted by Winterhalter at a State function in the Castle, wears a version of the uniform not far removed in style from the standard evening dress of today. He wears, moreover, a type of trousers known as overalls. This garment, first made fashionable by the Russian troops in London in 1814, and fastening beneath the boots, was by then well established. The first monarch to be painted in them was William IV, in his portrait by Shee.

When we come, in our view of male fashions, to neckwear, it is interesting in these portraits to trace the evolution of the seventeenth-century cravat down to the present-day tie. The cravat, so-called because it was introduced by the Croatian Guard of Louis XIV, replaced the neck-high lace collars of Van Dyck's Charles I and Charles II. It was at first a straight narrow strip of lace or linen, hanging down from the neck. In the eighteenth century the jabot took over, the ruffled and embroidered shirt-front billowing up over the opening of the waistcoat almost to conceal the neckcloth, which now buttoned at the back. Then the neckcloth re-established itself over the jabot, covering the shirt-front and evolving into the stock, which grew freer and more voluminous in its proportions as time went on.

Sir Thomas Lawrence's portraits of the Rulers and their Statesmen at the Congress of Vienna in 1814, which hang in the Waterloo Gallery at Windsor, depict them wearing sumptuous neckcloths, tied either in a bow or in a long turn-over knot. But it was Beau Brummell who first elevated the cravat into a cult—that crony and sartorial arbiter of George IV who was known to have reduced his king to tears by his criticism of the style of his costume.

Books were even written at this period with such titles as *The Art of Tying the Cravat*. Brummell was the first to introduce starch into it, insisting that it should be stiffened to the 'consistency of fine writing paper'. His dressing-room was, as Sir Max Beerbohm recalls, 'a studio in which he daily composed that elaborate portrait of himself which was to be exhibited for a few hours in the clubrooms of the town'. He would change his clothes three times a day, taking three hours over the process each time, and a number of these hours were devoted to tying and retying his cravats, discarding them and often spoiling them one after the other until knot and folds achieved that degree of immaculate perfection which the standards of the dandy demanded. Cravats, at this period, were sometimes as much as a foot high, with the points of the collars rising half-way up the face and obliging gentlemen to keep their chins and their heads well up in the air.

As the century went on, the cravats, as my family albums show, grew more casual again, while the collars became lower, with wide enough gaps between the points to allow the head to move freely enough from side to side. Lord Byron, with his loose open collars, proclaimed a reaction against 'Brummellism' towards a more comfortable form of neckwear. A portrait of him painted by Sandars, in a Highland scene, shows his cravat, knotted in a careless bow, flowing away from his neck in the breeze, in fine romantic style. Baron Stockmar, on the other hand, as befits the courtier as opposed to the poet, fancies himself, when sitting for his portrait by Partridge, in a cravat of the same kind, but more elegantly and discreetly tied.

The neckcloths of the Victorians remained ample and careless enough until the latter part of the century, when my grandfather, then starting to be a leader of fashion, came to prefer a more formally-tied stock, whether the 'four-in-hand' or the Ascot. Then the narrower types of necktie, the Derby, and the Oxford, began to make their appearance, foreshadowing the ties of today, with those smaller knots which give the collar more prominence.

The influence of Brummell, however, prevailed as it does still, in that all men now dressed more or less alike, with little of the eccentricity that prevailed in previous centuries. That it grew more and more sober in colour was due in the first place, perhaps, to Bulwer Lytton, that 'blighted being' who, as Mr. James Laver has pointed out, was the first man to wear nothing but black in the evening; and the blackness had spread to day clothes by the second half of the century.

It was relieved, however, in one respect. For now the new material of tweed came into vogue. By the 'seventies it had become fashionable to wear tweed trousers with dark frock- and morning-coats—and, indeed, even to wear morning-coats and jackets made of tweed.

People are wearing them still, in the pages of the family albums, when I make my own modest entrance into the world in the otherwise Naughty 'Nineties.

CHAPTER III

CHILDHOOD

Of all the old retainers whose unenviable task it was to look after me in childhood, only one survives. She is our old Nannie, who is known to me as Lala and to the rest of the world as Charlotte Bill. Like all head nurses and housekeepers of those days, she was accorded the courtesy title of Mrs. Lala was not present, it is true, to greet me on my entrance into the world in 1894. It was a year or so later that she came to us as nurse to my sister Mary and afterwards to my brothers. But she remembers very well the first clothes that I wore, layers of long flowing robes of cambric and muslin and lace.

Though now eighty-six years old, Lala is still as lively in her mind and as quick in her responses as ever. Only a few years ago she went on a cruise to South America, with her friend Mabel Butcher, who had been housekeeper at Sandringham. When I offered, before her departure, to teach her a few words of Spanish, she turned the offer down flat. 'What would I want with Spanish,' she inquired of me, 'at *my* age?'

Today Lala deplores, as she looks back, those clothes we were condemned to wear as babies. The weight of them was tiring to the right arm, however strong, of the nurse who had to carry us, and indeed to the baby itself. She treasures a photograph of Queen Victoria, holding one of my brothers in her arms and surrounded by other members of her family. She reveals that there was an invisible figure in the group when the photograph was taken—that of Lala herself, crouching behind to support the baby with her own arm, in case its weight should prove too much of a burden to the aged Queen. Lala it was who was really 'holding the baby'. She has also a photograph, blown up to the dimensions of a sizeable oil-painting, of my youngest brother John, dressed like some beautiful doll, with the skirts of two voluminous petticoats, one of flannel and the other of muslin, emerging from beneath his cambric frock, and with thick white stockings and tight buttoned boots encasing his legs and feet.

It was the rule, at the time of my babyhood, that a nurse must carry the baby in her arms for the first three months of its life, and if she neglected to do so she was regarded as no good at her job. The reason for this I cannot imagine: a superstition, perhaps, that the jolting of a perambulator would be harmful to the baby. Though I have no personal experience in such matters, I imagine that nowadays the little creatures are flung straight into a pram from the moment of birth, with as few clothes as possible to impede their movements. 'Nowadays,' as Lala puts it, 'they don't know they're born.'

Lala has vivid if not altogether agreeable memories of the nursery at York Cottage, Sandringham, in which we were obliged to spend our early years. 'The day nursery,' she declares, indicating with a wave of the hand her modest suburban living-room, 'was only about half as big as this. There was very little room for toys in it. You had only one small-sized rocking-horse. Perhaps it was a good thing your sister didn't go for dolls. They would have cluttered the place up terribly.'

These restrictions of our early environment were aggravated, at Frogmore, by the stuffiness of the rooms in which we spent part of the summer. They were right up under the roof, which was of the best quality lead—as we learned very soon when we took to clambering about on it—but on hot summer days had to be sprayed with water to prevent us from stifling. Some years before her death, my mother remarked to Lala, apropos the changes in habits of upbringing: 'Nurseries don't seem to be of much use any more. Nowadays the children are all over the house.' But that was not for my childhood.

Lala used to have a hard time with my father, who had strict views as to the correct conduct of children. 'Can't you stop that child crying?' he would bark at her irritably, especially when I was being taken to see my great-grandmother at Windsor. I was a nervous child, she maintains; sensing what was in store for me, I would start to cry the moment I was led from our rooms at the Castle, and I would seldom leave off until the audience was over. Understandably, this unaffectionate greeting displeased the Queen, who would vent her irritation on Lala. 'You had to mind your step,' she recalls, 'with Queen Victoria.'

When out of my baby clothes, Lala handed me over to the care of the faithful Frederick Finch, since departed, who features so prominently in the early part of my memoirs. I was now into kilts and sailor suits, which my father regarded as the only appropriate dress for children. His standards in this respect were strict. 'I hope your kilts fit well,' he wrote to me once at Balmoral, when I was nine years old. 'Take care and don't spoil them at once as they are new. Wear the Balmoral kilt and grey jacket on weekdays and green kilt and black jacket on Sundays. Do not wear the red kilt till I come.'

We were, in fact, figuratively speaking, always on parade, a fact that he would never allow us to forget. If we appeared before him with our Navy lanyards a fraction of an inch out of place, or with our dirks or sporrans awry, there would be an outburst worthy of the quarter-deck of a warship. Another greeted the appearance of one of us—it may well have been me—with hands stuffed into trouser pockets. Lala was immediately summoned and ordered to sew up the pockets of all our sailor suits, a royal command which, despite some inward reservations, she did not dare to disobey.

Constriction was the order of our schoolroom costume. We had a buttoned-up childhood, in every sense of the word. Starched Eton collars invariably encircled our necks and, when old and frayed, cut into our skin like saws. The idea of a boy in shirt sleeves and an open-necked collar was unthinkable. If, for some especial exertion, we were permitted to roll up our sleeves, we must still never loosen our collars and never take our coats off. Even with shorts we wore long stockings, right up to our thighs, with never a thought of anything so indelicate as bare knees—except in a kilt.

In one of my albums I have a photograph of my brother Bertie and me, in a group of a football team of

The Prince of Wales, later to be Edward VII, photographed in 1861 wearing a frock-coat. It was unusual for the slip and cravat to be of the same material as shown in the picture

Seen with a shooting party, the Prince of Wales is wearing corduroy plus-fours, a popular shooting costume of the 1870s

A Victorian garden-party scene with the Prince of Wales in a grey frock-coat and topper

Four generations in the Royal Family. A formal portrait of Queen Victoria with her eldest son, the Prince of Wales (later to be Edward VII), and myself still wearing skirts. Behind them is Princess Victoria of Wales, one of King Edward's daughters

My father, George V, then Prince George of Wales, wearing the uniform of a midshipman in the Royal Navy in 1879

My grandfather, the Prince of Wales in the 1880s in Highland Dress. The kilt was lower at that time than is normally worn

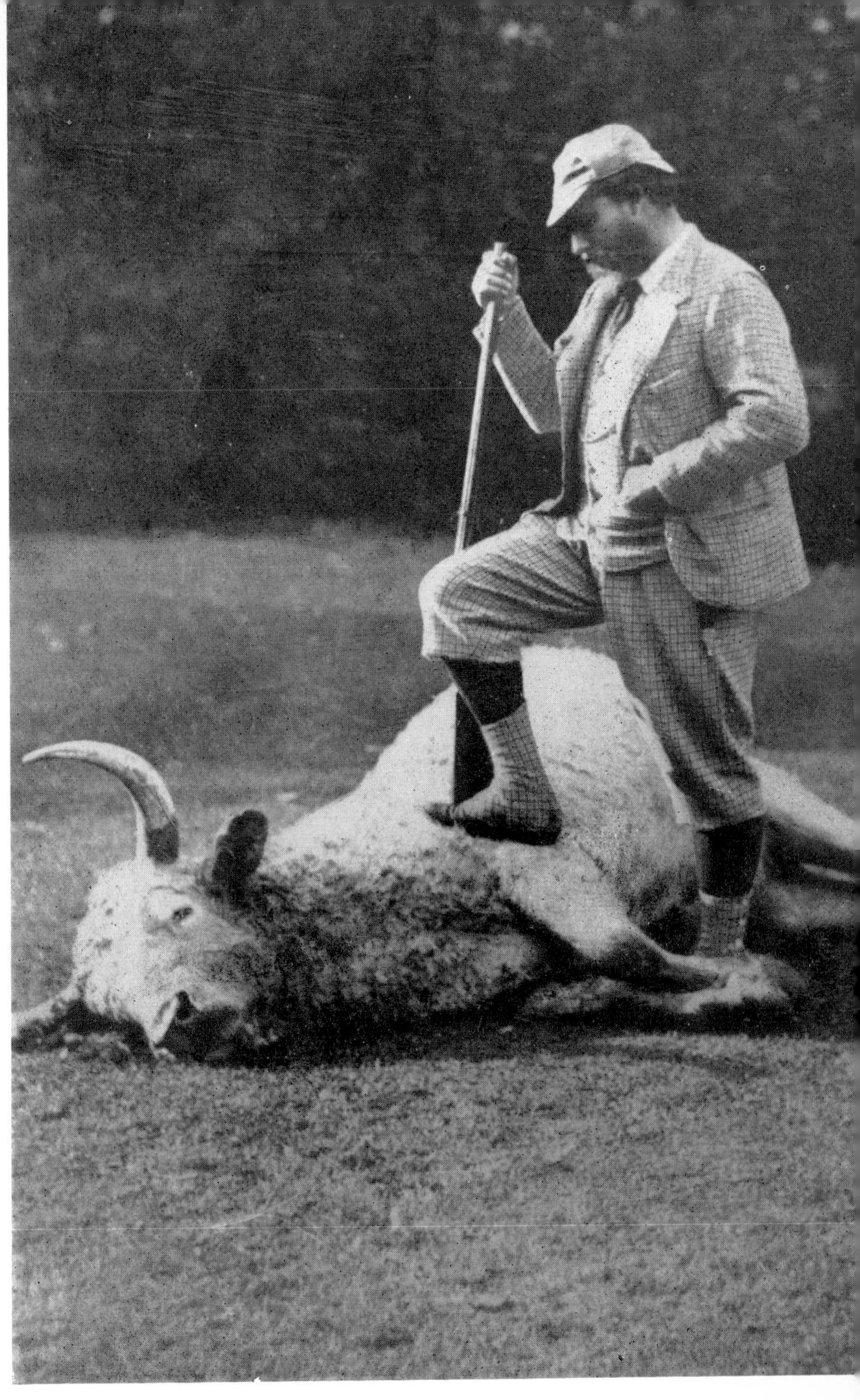

The Prince of Wales in the shooting costume of the 1880s. The gaiters and deerstalker cap were made of the same material as the plus-fours and jacket

The Prince and Princess of Wales, later to be Edward VII and Queen Alexandra, taken with their family in 1888. Seated at the foot with his sister is my father, George V (then Prince George), and standing beside him is his elder brother the Duke of Clarence (who died in 1891), here wearing the prominent collars and cuffs after which he was nick-named

Norfolk village boys. All of us are wearing knickerbockers, with long thick stockings—hardly a suitable costume in which to play this strenuous game with freedom. Another photograph shows us in a cricket group, with some boys of Mr. Gibbs's school—all of us with ties tied tightly around our necks.

My grandfather and his generation appeared to be more fortunate in this respect. He enjoyed his sailor suits, flaunting them before his governess and boasting in French, 'I'm a little cabin-boy. . . .'—moreover stuffing his hands into their pockets, as his portrait by Winterhalter shows. A photograph shows him at the age of twelve, dressed rather as a miniature grown-up than as a child, in black jacket, checked trousers and a fancy waistcoat, but with, as a concession to childhood, a comfortably loose Byronic collar and a floppy cravat. At Windsor I used to envy the children of George III, as portrayed by Gainsborough, wearing blouses wide open at the neck.

Such restraint in our clothes as we, by comparison, had to endure, has come to symbolize, in my mind, my early life and indeed some of my later life as well. My father and his generation, except when in the country, remained imprisoned in frock-coats and boiled shirts. I myself, on the other hand, as I grew up, developed in costume an urge towards greater freedom, and an adaptability to changing fashions. I broke to some extent the bonds of sartorial tradition. But always, in doing so, I incurred reprimands from that frock-coated enclave, the Palace. It is therefore hardly surprising that, on my Accession to the Throne, one of my first actions was to abolish the frock-coat for wear at Court.

But this happy emancipation was still a long way ahead. Meanwhile I was to face the alarming experience of going to school. The regulations of those Naval colleges at Osborne and Dartmouth were to condemn me, together with some hundreds of fellow cadets, to a stretch of four long years of boyhood in uniform, spent partly in quarters which had once been Queen Victoria's stables. The wardrobe—or 'gear' as I soon learnt to call it—with which I must now, at the age of twelve and a half, be equipped, was as follows:

1 White counterpane.
6 Sheets.
6 Pillow-cases.
1 Uniform jacket.
1 ,, trousers.
1 ,, waistcoat.
1 Flannel-lined waistcoat for the winter months.
2 Uniform caps, peak half-turned down.
1 Working summer suit, blue tweed, with two pairs of trousers.
1 Working winter suit of special material.
1 Loose-fitting overcoat—monkey jacket (to serve as overcoat at Osborne, and winter monkey jacket at Dartmouth).
1 Overcoat.
4 Pairs white flannel trousers, well-shrunk.
6 White flannel shirts (with collar turned down).
6 White day shirts.
12 Collars.
3 Pyjama suits.
8 Pairs Merino socks.
6 ,, thick woollen socks.
4 Pairs thin Merino drawers (short).

4 Pairs thick drawers for winter.
4 Thick vests for winter.
4 Bath towels.
4 Face towels.
1 Sweater (high in the neck).
2 Black silk neckties of uniform pattern.
12 Pocket-handkerchiefs.
2 Pairs white woollen gloves.
2 Pairs braces.
3 Pairs strong laced boots, soles at least ¾ in. thick.
1 Pair Oxford shoes, patent leather with strong soles.
1 Pair uniform gaiters.
1 Hair-brush.
1 Comb.
1 Clothes-brush.
1 Tooth-brush.
1 Nail-brush.
1 Sponge.
2 Soiled linen bags with name.
1 rug of uniform pattern.
1 Portmanteau or trunk with name.
1 Travelling bag with initials.
1 Key-bag with name.

Trousers, it was laid down, must be made without pockets—a deprivation to which I was already well broken in. Our monkey jackets were allowed two, an outside pocket on the left breast and an inside one on the right, but no side pockets. Only in our underwear did we have a glorious freedom of choice, with no pattern imposed. Government bedding was supplied (not including counterpane, sheets or pillow-cases). But for this we had to pay a shilling per month, while other articles, such as overalls, white football shorts, linen cricketing hats and broad straw boaters with a Navy ribbon, were charged to our personal accounts—that is to say, those of our parents. All this gear had to be kept in a wooden iron-bound sea-chest, 'complete with name in full engraved on a plain brass plate. Length 3 ft. 6 in.; breadth 2 ft.; height 2 ft. 3 in.' How it all fitted in there I cannot imagine; but it had to.

In my letters home from school, I was always careful to reassure my father as to my attention to dress. From Osborne I wrote:

> Mr. Gieve came down to try on a pair of new trousers for Cowes week, which are made the same size as my last ones, and they were 2 inches too big for me so that I am 2 inches thinner than when I first came here, which is a good thing I think.

From Dartmouth:

> Davies came down on Tuesday to try my clothes on, and Captain Napier kindly gave us a room in his house, where it could be done quietly. They are very smart indeed; two knickerbocker suits, and two walking suits. Davies told me that he was going to see you on Saturday, so he will tell you about it.

I knew also that my haircuts were a matter of some concern to him. Thus I wrote:

> I think I shall get my hair cut a little at the back, as it looks rather bad.

Faced with the prospect of confronting his critical eye at the end of term, I wrote from Osborne:

> My hair is very long so do you think I ought to get it trimmed before I leave here? But I am afraid Moon will spoil it. I shall be in London on Thursday, when Charles will cut it properly. Could you let me know as soon as possible?

This 'Charles' was an Austro-Hungarian barber who had been established, under the aegis of my grandfather, in a shop on Piccadilly, and was widely patronized by his friends and the *élite* of British Society. My father dutifully became one of Charles's clients, but rebelled when he eventually discovered that he was being grossly overcharged. He transferred his patronage to an English barber named Charles Topper, who cut his hair and beard until the end of his life.

My letter brought forth a telegram from Elveden, in Suffolk, where my father was shooting, followed by a letter:

> I think it would be much better to wait till you come home to have your hair cut by Charles, which you can do on Thursday—Moon will only spoil it.

Fortunately for poor Moon, this message never reached the eye of the College authorities, while he was still their barber. His reputation would have been ruined, and he would surely have lost his job.

Another fatherly epistle ran:

> I hope your hair has grown properly now, I hear the stupid man had cut it all off.

That was before the days of the crew-cut—the fashion of clipping the hair close which, as a hangover from the last war, has been adopted by so much of the youth of America.

CHAPTER IV

GRANDFATHER

My grandfather began, from his early youth, to do the wrong thing in the critical eyes of his father and mother—rather as his grandson was to do in the eyes of his, later on. Having obeyed, no doubt, their injunctions as to the significance of dress for a prince, his reward, at the age of seventeen, was a sharp comment from the Prince Consort to the Princess Royal: 'Unfortunately, he takes no interest in anything but clothes, and again clothes. Even when out shooting, he is more occupied with his trousers than with the game!'

A year later, when he was entertaining the city fathers at Holyrood Palace in Edinburgh, General Bruce remarked to the Queen on the poignant contrast between the portly grey-haired guests and the faintly epicene beauty of their adolescent host. The Queen promptly wrote to order her son to give up his practice of wearing slippers and 'loose long jacket', and to part his hair in a less 'girlish and effeminate way'. This was distinctly unfair in view of the fact that the Prince Consort was remarkable, according to Thomas Carlyle, for the 'loose greyish clothes' that he wore.

My great-grandfather could hardly claim to be an arbiter of fashion. For shooting he used to wear a black velvet jacket and long scarlet boots, a costume which the Queen found 'very picturesque'. But it must have aroused some derision from the British country gentry who, according to Lytton Strachey, regarded the Prince Consort as looking 'more like some foreign tenor'. The Prince Consort was partial to velvet. Queen Victoria recalled him thus at breakfast on their honeymoon: 'He wore a black velvet jacket without a cravat and anything more beautiful—and more youthfully manly and perfect—never was seen.'

King Edward himself, as Prince of Wales, later adopted this fashion, introducing a velvet suit, with a loose jacket and trousers for wear in country houses. In the world of Elinor Glyn, the gentlemen vied with one another in the brightness of their velvet jackets, which they wore for tea, flaunting colours that ranged from turquoise blue to emerald green and crimson. But I fancy this did not last long in what were known as the 'best' country houses. Oscar Wilde used to lecture in a velvet suit, presenting a spectacle which, I have little doubt, helped to hasten the death of this fashion.

King Edward was essentially manly in his costume, whatever his mother may have thought and said. He was a dandy in his way, such as the Prince Consort might have regarded as 'frivolous' and 'foolish', but in fact infinitely less so than the dandies of George IV's time. His clothes, as I remember from my youth, were always elegant, fitting tight at the waist. But they were so well cut that they were somehow able to conceal the fact that he had lost his figure years before. He never gave the impression of being, in fact, a very fat man.

His collars, shirt-fronts and cuffs were stiff with starch. Not a detail was out of place, from the white rims of the spats around the ankles of his well-polished boots, to the white cuffs at his wrists and the white slip around the neck of his well-fitting waistcoat. Not a button was unfastened, save perhaps the bottom button of the waistcoat. The undoing of this button became a fashion which has persisted to this day, but I rather suspect he may have, in the first place, left it undone by mistake.

He also had a taste and flair for uniforms, which this grandson of his was not to inherit. Admiral of the Fleet, Field-Marshal, moreover Colonel-in-Chief of many British regiments, besides foreign ones, he would be consulted on any proposed change in the dress regulations of the forces. None were made without his approval, and it was said that he displayed a keener sense of proportion and detail than any of the General Officers on the Committee appointed to consider reforms in Army dress after the last Boer War.

One of these reforms concerned the controversial 'Brodrick Cap'—named for St. John Brodrick, later Earl of Midleton, then Secretary of State for War. Its invention was attributed to my grandfather. Prescribed for undress wear in place of the old 'pill-box' cap, it was essentially German in design and, because it had no peak to protect the eyes, was unpopular among the other ranks of the British Army. It was abolished in favour of peaked caps after King Edward's death in 1910, except for the Royal Marines, who wore it for another ten years.

It was the custom, before the First World War, for European rulers to confer upon each other honorary ranks or appointments, *à la suite* to various regiments, in each other's armies or navies. Thus my grandfather and my father had several foreign uniforms, while the continental monarchs of the time had British ones. On one of Kaiser Wilhelm II's visits to Queen Victoria in England he conferred upon my grandfather another honorary German military rank, naturally expecting a British one in return. For the sake of diplomatic harmony, the old Queen complied, but in a letter she wrote with some asperity: 'This fishing for uniforms on both sides is regrettable.'

My grandfather, however, never took uniforms as seriously as did the Kaiser who, following the practice at other Continental courts, wore a uniform at all times. In fact he was seldom seen in plain clothes, in which he never felt at ease, and he wore them badly. He had even devised a '*Jagd* uniform' for shooting. This was a dark green 'Loden' suit of jacket and knickerbockers, worn with high black boots. It had an ornate leather belt, from which hung an elaborate short sword, and a stiff green Homburg hat surmounted by long dark feathers completed the outfit. I remember he and his *Jägers* wearing this costume for shooting at Sandringham, to the consternation of the Norfolk yokels who were hired as beaters.

King Edward is said to have been more amused than sympathetic when the Kaiser complained to him officially that Mr. John Montagu had received him at Beaulieu, disrespectfully dressed in a blue serge suit and a bowler hat. Mr. Montagu (afterwards Lord Montagu of Beaulieu) replied, when this complaint was relayed to him by the Foreign Office, that he had been accustomed to receiving King Edward in similar garb, and that what was good enough for the King of England was surely good enough for the Kaiser.

The Kaiser himself slipped up in his dress when he arrived at Osborne for the funeral of Queen Victoria, without a pair of black trousers. But he was saved by the local tailor, who made him a pair in a few hours—and next day put up the Royal Warrant sign before his shop. King Edward once slipped up when, with Queen Alexandra, he visited the Tsar and Tsarina of Russia at Reval in 1906. He had neglected to try on in advance the Russian uniform procured for the occasion, and when he put it on found it so tight that he could not button it without acute discomfort. A Russian tailor was summoned, but he could not alter it in time. So the King had to go aboard the Imperial yacht bursting out of his uniform, and not in the best of humours.

The cult of the uniform spread even to democratic Belgium, where I was once the guest of the late King Albert at Laaken. Noticing that he was always dressed in military khaki, I finally asked him: 'Sir, do you always wear uniform?' 'Yes,' was his reply. 'You see, my wife does not find that I look well in civilian clothes.' I believe the Queen was right.

Although I was never so interested in uniforms as my grandfather, I became used to them by force of circumstance during the First World War and in the course of my official duties afterwards. I took a special pride in the uniform of the Brigade of Guards, whose most distinctive feature is the famous bearskin cap. Oddly enough this is not as uncomfortable a form of headgear as might be supposed, once it is properly 'broken in' to the head. I used to keep my head 'in training' for the bearskin, by wearing it in moments of leisure and privacy during week-ends at the Fort.

When my brother the Duke of York was appointed Colonel of the Scots Guards and thus had to wear a bearskin for the first time, I strongly advised him to follow my example. Unfortunately he chose to disregard my advice, remarking: 'I have tried it on and it seems to fit perfectly well.' Retribution fell upon him not long afterwards at the King's Birthday parade. The cap began to give him such pain that he was obliged to withdraw from the parade, dismounting and relieving his head for a while before he could return and resume his place. Already piqued at this discomfiture, he was still less pleased when I afterwards chaffed him with the irresistible comment: 'I told you so!'

My grandfather unquestionably had a wider influence on masculine fashions than any member of the Royal Family since George IV. He was a good friend to the tailors of Savile Row, consolidating the position of London as the international sartorial shrine for men, as already Paris was for women. When he visited Marienbad—as he got into the habit of doing each year incognito as the Duke of Lancaster to 'take the waters'—tailors from Paris, Vienna and all parts of the Continent used to gather and to follow him around, surreptitiously photographing him and jotting down notes on his clothes. Prince von Bülow, the German Chancellor, in his memoirs described him as, in this sphere, the 'uncontested *arbiter elegantiarum*'.

'In the country,' he writes, 'in which unquestionably the gentlemen dressed best, he was the best-dressed gentleman. Few men since George IV and his friend Brummell have worn civilian clothes better.'

Prince von Bülow remembered the foremost tailor in Vienna, Herr Frank, admiring the King's trouser crease. 'Personally,' he admits, 'I was unable properly to appreciate the supreme importance of this crease, but Herr Frank, a gentleman not only as regards his perfectly-cut clothes but also by nature, thought a lot of it. The Germans were inclined to mock at the King's preoccupation with clothes, but this von Bülow thought it 'politically silly'. The Kaiser, after all, changed his uniforms quite as often as the King changed his suits.

King Edward's ministers and associates came to fear his criticism and sarcasm in relation to their dress, whether uniform or otherwise. There is a familiar story that when Lord Rosebery appeared at Windsor Castle for some official ceremony, wearing plain clothes and knee-breeches instead of full dress uniform, the King admonished him with the words: 'I presume you have come in the suite of the American Ambassador.'

To Disraeli, when he appeared as one of the Elder Brethren of Trinity House, wearing Diplomatic uniform with his Trinity House trousers, he remarked jocularly: 'It won't do. You're found out.' The attire of the Cecils, traditionally careless, always shocked him exceedingly. Thanking the Duke of Devonshire for a party at Devonshire House, he remarked that only one thing was wrong. 'What was that?' the Duke asked anxiously. The King replied: 'You've got your Garter on upside down.'

From his early youth, he developed a keen sense of style and of cut. One night, as Prince of Wales, he went to the theatre to see the French actor, Fechter, play

Robert Macaire. The adventurer's coat, in the piece, was a mass of rents and patches, but the acute royal eye quickly noticed that the garment was well cut, and at the end of the play he sent for the actor and asked him the name of his tailor. The answer was Poole, and from that day Poole became the Prince's chief tailor. When he died in 1876, a New York paper published his epitaph:

> Yes, Poole's my tailor. Poole! You know!
> Who makes the Prince of Wales's things.
> He's tailor (as his billheads show) to
> half the Emperors and Kings.
> An introduction is required
> At Poole's before they take your trade.
> No common people are desired
> However promptly bills are paid.

My grandfather's ample frame became unsuited, as he grew older, to open or cutaway jackets. Thus his coat was inevitably the frock-coat, straight and broad and massive. Double-breasted at first, it became, as he grew more portly, single-breasted—but unobtrusively so, since it was cut in the same way, with double-breasted lapels. It could be fastened in front, and for this he chose an onyx link button. For less formal occasions he would wear the double-breasted 'reefer' jacket, which thus became popular. Of naval origin, and worn for yachting, it was the ancestor of the double-breasted lounge jacket of today, but cut higher at the neck.

My grandfather was one of the first to introduce a crease into the trousers—a crease that ran sideways, not frontways like the creases of today. Hitherto trousers had been worn uncreased, sometimes folding around the instep or strapped beneath the foot, but becoming increasingly loose. When tweeds came in, the lack of a crease gave them a baggy unkempt look, familiar in Victorian photographs.

There are various stories as to the origin of the crease, of which the most picturesque—doubtless apocryphal—recounts that my grandfather once had a fall from his horse, and was taken to a cottage to rest while his clothes were dried and pressed. The flurried cottager pressed the trousers with a crease at the sides, and the King liked the fashion and thenceforward followed it.

More probably the crease dates from the introduction of the trouser-press, around the turn of the century, or arose naturally from the habit of folding trousers, when men grew tidier in their dress. Even so, the crease did not establish itself immediately. As late as 1907 the tailors were trying to defy the trouser-press makers by making trousers with a dent in the material just above the boot, to hold their shape.

Another of my grandfather's innovations was the low-cut, white waistcoat for wear with a dress-coat. This exposed for the first time a really substantial expanse of shirt-front, and benefited shirt-makers and laundrymen alike. Stiff as a breast-plate across the manly chest, this shirt-front was nevertheless vulnerable. My grandfather found it so one evening, when my mother and father were dining with him and my grandmother at Buckingham Palace, before going on to the opera. The menu included a *purée* of spinach, and the King was unfortunate enough to spill a gobbet of this vegetable on his wide and spotless shirt.

Queen Alexandra took a knife and tried to scrape it off.

My mother also did her best to repair the damage. But the tell-tale mark remained, and it now became obvious that he would be obliged to change his shirt. Instead of getting mad, as he would have been entitled to do, he laughed boisterously, dipped his napkin in the spinach, and drew a picture with it all over the shirt-front—an abstract painting in spinach, in the style which on the Left Bank in Paris today is, I believe, called Tachiste. Then he went to change, and this royal work of art was lost for ever.

Hard-shirted and hard-collared, my grandfather was also hard-hatted. His formal attire was completed by the top hat, which he and my father wore not only on all occasions in London but for church on Sundays in the country; or else by the bowler hat, which by the end of his reign had begun seriously to undermine the supremacy of the top hat. The bowler was first made by a Mr. Bowler of Houndsditch, London, to the specification of William Coke, a Norfolk squire of the family of the Earls of Leicester. It was thus nicknamed the Billy Coke, or Billycock, and to this day Lock's, the St. James's hatters, refer to it as a William Coke hat. It was originally designed for country and sporting wear only. Until after my grandfather's time, it was considered unthinkable to wear it in London. But he helped to give it an urban character, thus spiting that stern arbiter of male fashion the *Tailor and Cutter*, which was raging against the bowler hat even as late as 1909, as 'an abomination in head covering. Men of individuality eschew it and never give it peg-room in their hat-stand'.

From the conventional black bowler hat my grandfather evolved a grey variety, for summer wear, and even wore a brown one which crossed to America where it became the 'Brown Derby' and was made famous by Governor Al Smith of New York State. So popular did it become over there that a chain of restaurants was named for it, still retaining the name today. Once at Baden Baden my grandfather startled his compatriots by wearing a bowler with a tail-coat, a continental fashion much derided by the British. He also sported the half top hat made of hard felt, like a bowler, which Sir Winston Churchill still wears. Once a favourite of farmers, who called it a 'cheerer', it was the inspiration of the *Daily Mail* hat which that newspaper tried, without success, to introduce in the nineteen-twenties.

It was from Germany that King Edward introduced the Homburg hat. He discovered this on a visit to a felt-hat factory in Homburg, where he acquired a number of specimens for himself and his friends. In England he wore the hat first at a race meeting, and soon the aforesaid arbiter of fashion was referring with interest to 'the stock of felts' he had brought back from Marienbad. Soft though the felt was, it still looked like a hard hat, when perched on my grandfather's head, and it had a curled braided brim, not unlike that of a bowler. He sometimes wore a black version of it, like the so-called 'Anthony Eden' hat, which was revived for Foreign Office wear some twenty years later by Lord Curzon.

King Edward thus reintroduced gaiety into the Court not merely in the social but in the sartorial sense. This was evident especially in his colourful country clothes. Having a leg hardly suitable for breeches, he wore knickerbockers instead, not tapering to the knee in the accepted fashion, but bagging a little over it, and thus fathering the plus-fours of a later generation. He wore

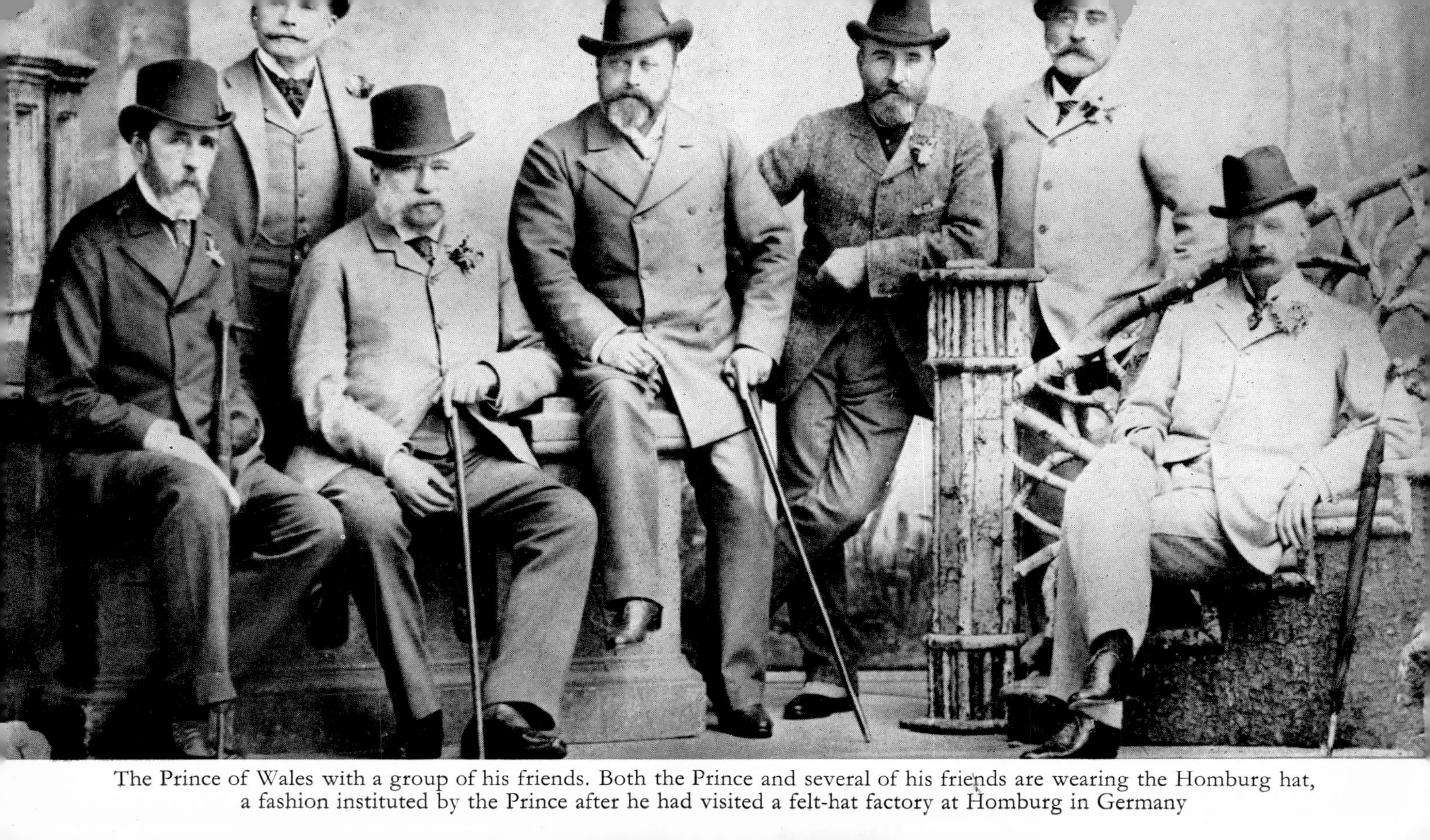

The Prince of Wales with a group of his friends. Both the Prince and several of his friends are wearing the Homburg hat, a fashion instituted by the Prince after he had visited a felt-hat factory at Homburg in Germany

A bicycling party in 1883. The two young men in pill-box hats are my father and, seated on one of the bicycles, Prince

The Prince of Wales in 1898. His trousers do not have a crease, and the bottom button of his waistcoat has been left undone

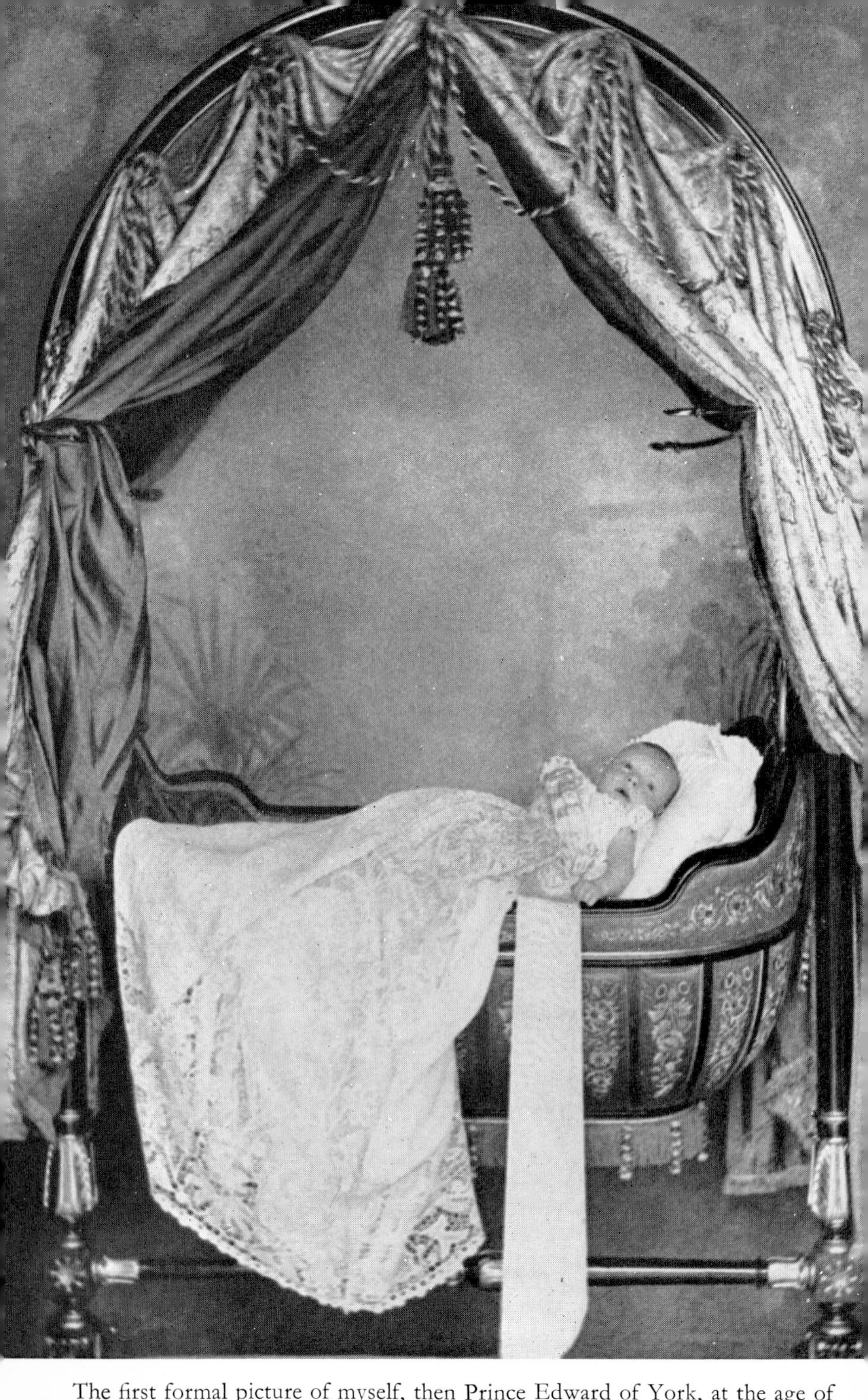

The first formal picture of myself, then Prince Edward of York, at the age of about six weeks

Another early photograph, taken on my first birthday in 1895

A picture of Queen Alexandra, then Princess of Wales, with her two sons Prince Albert Victor and Prince George, my father, taken in Scotland

A similar picture of my mother at the time when she was Princess of Wales, with Bertie and myself wearing the same Balmoral tartan as in the previous picture. There is a thirty-year gap between these two groups, so similar in spirit and costume

Charlotte Bill, who is now aged eighty-five, with two attendant nursesmaids and her royal charges

these for shooting, made of bold checked tweeds, with bright-patterned stockings, which he wore with spats stretching almost up the knee. Over all this he would often wear a voluminous Inverness cape, also made of tweed. In my album I have a characteristic photograph of him in this garment, riding on a pony and smoking a large cigar. He even adapted it to evening dress, having it made in black, lining it with silk and wearing it like an opera cloak. My father had one of these capes, of the tweeded variety, which I inherited at his death and which I sometimes wear today, once provoking the exclamation 'Sherlock Holmes!' from a French security officer assigned to me.

In his liking for colour in clothes, my grandfather sometimes overdid the effect, as when a (doubtless Anglophobic) French newspaper described him at Marienbad as wearing 'a green cap, a brown overcoat, and pink necktie, grey shoes, white gloves and knee-breeches'. On this, the tailoring Press commented with a certain asperity: 'We sincerely hope His Majesty has not brought this outfit home.'

This bright tweeded opulence of my grandfather and his friends, while out shooting at Sandringham, was always a wonder to me as a child. But they and my father wore even their tweeds, as they did their other clothes, not with a view to relaxation but as a costume dictated by custom for a particular purpose. Each activity of theirs called for its especial attire, hence for frequent changes of clothes during a single day. If, for example, my father were driving down to Windsor from London in the afternoon, he would still put on his town morning clothes in the morning, and only change into his country clothes after luncheon. After an afternoon's shooting, he would invariably change from his tweeds into another suit—often a velvet or a tartan suit—for the ceremony of tea, a ritual repast of importance to the hungry British.

Once, after shooting at Sandringham, I had gone to the kennels to look after one of my dogs, who was sick, and appeared for tea still dressed in my shooting clothes. This brought me an immediate reprimand from my father, in front of a number of guests, for being improperly dressed. I immediately left the tea-table and, stung by his attitude, ordered tea for myself in my room, arguing with him afterwards that I was now, at the age of thirty, old enough to please myself in such matters, at least in the family home and in an age when such rigid dress conventions no longer prevailed.

The country clothes of my father and grandfather showed little of that easy looseness familiar in sports clothes today. Their shirts may have been soft, and even sometimes coloured, but their collars were still invariably starched, and so generally remained until the First World War.

At Sandringham I remember also the uniforms of the gamekeepers. They wore bowler hats with gold cords round the base of the crown, and gold lace acorns on the front. But the head-keeper wore one of these half top hats, a 'cheerer', and carried a silver horn—on a cord of red braid with tassels slung over his green brass-buttoned coat of Melton cloth. The other keepers wore coats of green velveteen, introduced by the Prince Consort from Germany, with brass buttons, while their breeches were of tight cord, worn with gaiters.

This picturesque outfit persisted, with some modifications, right up to the end of my father's reign. But it was changed by my brother. Today the keepers wear an ordinary green tweed, with boots, stockings and anklets, and green felt hats. Today it is only at Holkham, Lord Leicester's estate, that the gamekeepers still wear bowler hats. The beaters, when I was young, used to wear smocks, and black felt hats with blue and red ribbons, known as 'chummies'. After the First World War they wore caps instead.

At Sandringham everything, including, I regret to say, the interests of the farmers, was subordinated to the shooting. In the library at Windsor I remember a book named *Eighteen Years on the Sandringham Estate*, written by 'The Lady Farmer'—in fact, a spirited widow named Mrs. Gerard Cresswell, the tenant of Appleton House. The agent at Sandringham was instructed by Sir Dighton Probyn to buy up and destroy copies of this book, which gave considerable offence to my grandfather. She records her continual guerrilla conflict with him over the harm done to her crops by his enormous operations for the rearing and destruction of game.

'The Lady Farmer' lost her battle in the end, and had to sell up her farm, while her house became the home of my aunt, Queen Maud of Norway. But she could still write, despite her grievances, of my grandfather's 'extraordinary charm of manner and power of putting everyone at their ease whether they might be driving a donkey-cart or cleaning a grate, without a suggestion of patronage or difference of rank'. She might have added 'difference of age'; he certainly knew how to put children at their ease. The 'Big House' under his auspices seemed to me, as a child, the quintessence of all that was amusing and gay.

CHAPTER V

OXFORD

It was not until I went, with a certain reluctance, up to Oxford that I myself attained to some degree of social and sartorial freedom. Here no rules were laid down as to what we should wear, though undergraduate costume was still more conservative than it became later on. Flannel trousers were the rule, and sports coats or blazers, and sometimes knickerbockers, which had grown baggier, expanding not yet into plus-fours but into plus-ones or plus-twos.

In terms of clothes, this was a very different Oxford from the University which my grandfather had known. We wore our waist-length undergraduate gowns for lectures only, and the traditional 'mortar-boards' hardly ever. King Edward, as Prince of Wales, who went both to Oxford and to Cambridge, was obliged, in deference to the wishes of his parents, to wear the full undergraduate regalia of a 'nobleman', namely a velvet cap with gold tassel and a long, full-sleeved black gown; and when he appeared in the Oxford Union all the undergraduates would rise respectfully to their feet. Such a costume was not inflicted on his eldest son, the Duke of Clarence, at Cambridge who wore the ordinary Commoner's gown; nor was he accorded such marks of respect. But he made up for this later on, I do not doubt, with those highly starched appurtenances which won him the name of 'Collars and Cuffs'.

At this undergraduate stage, after emerging from five years spent in naval uniform, I must have started to take a genuine interest in my clothes: but it was always in the informal sense. Photographs of the period portray me, posing with an air of superiority, as a youth-about-town, before my brothers, still in their schoolboy suits; wearing my hat at a rakish angle, tying my bow-tie with care, smoking a pipe or a cigarette as nonchalantly as any grown-up. Doubtless I fancied myself as a bit of a dandy—but, of course, of the discreetest possible kind.

King Edward, at this age, looked a dandy too, but cast in a more formal mould. Photographs of him at the age of twenty show an elegant, slim young man in an immaculate braided frock-coat, plaid trousers and a striped silk stock. He wears a watch-chain across his waistcoat and carries a cane and a high top hat, while his fair hair is of a length which, by my Oxford standards, would have been thought distinctly 'aesthetic'. It was this, no doubt, at which Queen Victoria had voiced her displeasure.

My correspondence with my father now dwelt less upon clothes and haircuts. Doubtless I had grown more emancipated in this respect. But I did touch on the theme, with a superior air, after a visit to Harrow:

I was not struck by the outward appearance of the Harrow boys, who are abominably dressed and slouch about in a shocking manner.

From Oxford I would now write, reassuring him as to the way I was reacting to other pitfalls of youth:

I never smoke more than ten cigarettes a day, generally not as many, and then only smoke in the evening after dinner with never more than two before tea. . . . I am also in bed by 10.30 almost every evening.

I must have improved upon this, for three months later he was writing to me:

Glad you only smoke 6 cigarettes a day, what about pipes?

The Times, as it happens, declared that I had on my arrival, 'overjoyed the tobacconists of Oxford, as well as other tradesmen, by falling an easy victim to the profusion of rare tobaccos, straight-grained pipes, and other cunningly designed or presumably useful articles which are spread forth as a snare for the solvent freshman'.

My drinking habits called for further reassurance to my father. Describing a Bullingdon Club dinner, at which sixty undergraduates were present, I wrote:

Most of them got rather, if not to say very, excited and I came back early. There was a good deal of champagne drunk and that accounted for it. It is interesting for me to see the various forms of amusement that undergraduates indulge in.

He replied, on the stationery of Welbeck Abbey:

> I was amused with your description of your dinner at the Bullingdon Club, it appears that a good many of the young men drank more champagne than was good for them and became very noisy and excited, different people have different ways of enjoying themselves.

I now recall with some shame that the real reason for my early departure from this entertainment was the fact that I was no longer so steady on my feet or so clear in my speech as I was when we sat down to dinner. I hasten to add that this was an unusual occurrence, prompted only by the unwritten law of the Bullingdon Club that the new members should be forced to drink themselves into oblivion. Later on, I had another experience of the pitfalls of drinking too well, at a 'wine' one evening, after dinner in the junior common-room at Magdalen. My tipple on that occasion was port, which has never tasted quite the same to me since. During the following vacation, in the sobriety of the family home, I wrote, a little self-righteously, to an Oxford friend, Jack Paterson:

> I hope you had a good week-end with Davies, and that he has absolutely recovered from that famous wine. I have not touched a drop of wine since I have been down and have no craving for it whatever. I think we have the same views on the subject.

At this time I had started to spend my vacations abroad, first in France and then in Germany, in order to learn the languages. In France, I was put through an intensive course of visits to museums, cathedrals and châteaux, which gave me a certain cultural indigestion. But I was happy to stay with my grandfather's old friends, the Marquis and Marquise de Breteuil, who were charming and considerate hosts, and under their auspices I made my début in French society. In a letter to my father, at the age of eighteen, I described my reactions to a dinner to which they took me, given by the Duc and Duchesse de Luynes at the Château de Dampierre:

> The only thing was that we sat down over 70 people to dinner, which was rather alarming as I knew barely 20 of them. But everybody walked about in the garden afterwards, so it was not so bad.

In their house in Paris and at the Château de Breteuil near Chevreuse—only a few miles away from our Mill in the next valley of the Meranthaise—the Marquis and the Marquise entertained much and lavishly. Their distinguished friends, although elegantly dressed, often appeared in costumes that were, to say the least, original. The old Marquis du Los wore a straw boater with a grey frock-coat, my French tutor Maurice Escoffier a bowler hat with a morning-coat, while, as elsewhere described, Detaille, the military artist, sported Black Watch tartan trousers with his morning-coat. Unlike Escoffier, however, he wore the correct top hat.

In my youth I felt more at home in Germany, largely because there I stayed mostly among relatives. On these visits I was accompanied by Dr. Hermann Fiedler, my German tutor at Oxford, with his flowing picturesque white moustache. I am ashamed to recall that on one occasion, anxious to sample the night life of Berlin with a friend unattended, I locked the worthy professor into his bathroom in the Hotel Esplanade, where we were stopping. But I did at least explain to the porter that I thought the lock of the bathroom had gone wrong—with the Herr Professor inside; and I gave him the key, so that Fiedler might be released when I was safely away.

In Germany almost everyone wore some kind of uniform—a fact which did not surprise me, from my boyhood experiences of the Kaiser in England. But I was forcibly reminded of this custom on my arrival at Stuttgart, during a vacation from Oxford, to stay with my uncle and aunt, the King and Queen of Württemberg. To my undergraduate friend, Jack Paterson, I wrote:

> My arrival here was humorous [*sic*]; oh yes, very much so. Of course, you know that nearly everyone in Germany wears uniform; I, having come a long way in the car, arrived appropriately attired for that pastime only was dusty and was wearing that famous light blue coat you know so well and a dirty old hat. Imagine my horror on crossing the threshold to find that the hall was full of officers in uniform!! The King, his family and staff, were falling over each other with swords, spurs, helmets and what not; so that I don't suppose I created a very favourable impression. I cat with laughter now when I think about it, but those first ten minutes here were a great strain!!

Meanwhile the spectre of 'uniform', from which I had been freed since leaving the Navy, had risen once again before me, with the approach of my majority at the age of eighteen in 1912. My father wrote to me in France:

> I have told Davies that you must have tights and a Windsor coat and white waistcoat made by the time you arrive at Windsor on the 21st.

By 'tights' my father was referring to knee-breeches and the 'Windsor' coat meant the Windsor Uniform. I was assuring him a few days before my birthday: 'I will bring my uniform for the inspection.'

The seal of approval on my clothes at this time was set by the *Tailor and Cutter*. On my arrival at Oxford in 1912, it recorded: 'There has been nothing daring or original in his sartorial equipment, but rather the unobtrusive shades and outlines that always distinguish the well-dressed gentleman'—a testimonial which might not have displeased the Prince Consort, or even Mr. Brummell himself. Previously, on spying me at the International Horse Show, this journal had remarked that, in matters of dress, I had 'so far displayed remarkably good taste in the selection of his tweed suits and mufti overcoats'.

At the wedding of my cousin, Prince Arthur of Connaught, I was described as 'attractively dressed in his naval uniform with the ribbon of the Garter', while later I was seen 'to have put on a frock-coat with silk facings on the lapel and a flower in his buttonhole'. How I must have hated it! How my father must have approved! How much more so after my first public ceremony—the consecration of a new church on the Duchy of Cornwall estate at Kennington—when; 'Following in the footsteps of his father, and also of his grandfather, he adopted the frock-coat for this public function, and so set the seal of approval on a garment which in recent years has been much decried.'

As a matter of fact, outside of Court circles, the frock-coat, I fancy, was already on the decline. It was now worn mainly by bank clerks and shop walkers—and, indeed, the clerks at Coutts's gentlemanly bank wear frock-coats to this day. The *Tailor and Cutter* was waging a losing battle in its favour—a battle to which it nevertheless reverted as late as the nineteen-thirties, when it chose to see a revival of the fashion in my father's continued loyalty to this formal and constricting garment.

In other respects, my costume at this period did not always please my father. He disapproved, as I have already recorded, of the 'cuffs' or turn-ups of my trouser legs. This practice, I dare say, was introduced casually at first, to protect trousers from the rain, and then crystallized into a fashion. In 1911 the *West End Gazette of Fashion* disapprovingly commented: 'Now, rain or shine, clear or stormy, there are found many "weaklings" who consider it *en règle* to have the bottoms of their trousers made permanently pressed turned up, so as to form a kind of loose cuff round their feet.'

Recently, in Britain and elsewhere, I have noticed a tendency to abandon these permanent sewn-up 'cuffs' on trousers. More conservative than I used to be, I still prefer the style I have worn for almost fifty years. But I dare say that some of my generation follow the youngsters, by reverting to the old fashion of 'no cuffs'. This would have pleased my father.

I know one of them, at least, who has done so—an old American friend and contemporary of mine. Not long ago he was spending the week-end at the Mill with his wife. He had just returned from a visit to his tailor in London, and I immediately noticed that his 'pants' were 'cuffless'. Chiding him on his fickleness in the matter of clothes, I sensed he was hurt that I had not approved the change. Anyway, next morning the laugh was on me. My friend had had his wife sew up the bottoms of his trousers to form a cuff one foot high, and so attired he accompanied me for a golf game.

When I look at the photographs of myself at this period just before the First World War, I notice how different in detail are the clothes I was wearing from those of the post-war age. My trousers are still narrow, of the drainpipe variety. My jackets are cut longer than those of today, and button higher at the top. My collars are still stiff. I invariably carry gloves and a cane. It was in fact this 'Edwardian' fashion that the tailors of Savile Row laudably tried to revive after the Second World War. The attempt failed, through the adoption of the changes by a less reputable section of society. This was, perhaps, a pity.

CHAPTER VI

FATHER

After my grandfather died, the character of the Court soon changed. Gone was its light-hearted cosmopolitan atmosphere. Buckingham Palace, Windsor Castle, Sandringham and Balmoral reverted to a way of life not, it is true, as austere as in Queen Victoria's time, but quieter, more sedate and more essentially British than that of the Edwardian age.

My grandfather had loved society, especially the society of women—so much so that at one time he abolished at Windsor the time-honoured British habit by which the ladies, after dinner, leave the gentlemen alone to their port. Instead, ladies and gentlemen would process out of the dining-room together, in continental fashion. This did not suit his ministers, who liked to have this opportunity for a word with him alone, perhaps on some matter of public affairs, and after a while he abandoned the practice, denying himself for this one half-hour the amenities of feminine company. When he went out, which he liked to do often, among a small circle of intimate friends, he preferred little dinners of four or eight or, at the most, twelve, invariably with bridge—and feminine partnership at the bridge-table—to follow.

My father always preferred masculine to feminine company. Moreover, he enjoyed his port and liked to drink it at his ease, when the ladies had gone. He was an abstemious man, preceding the port with only a single whisky and soda, drunk during dinner. Cocktails were unheard of in his houses, and it was impossible to order a drink of any kind outside of mealtimes. If my brothers and I required one, we would have to resort to a private supply which we kept in our rooms.

Nevertheless, it was a deprivation to my father, when, during the First World War, the Court, prompted by Lloyd George and as an example to the nation, went 'on the wagon'—or, as the British then called it, 'on the water-cart'. The doors of the cellars in his houses were locked for the 'duration', and no alcoholic liquor was served at the royal table or those of the Household and the servants. But after dinner my father would make an excuse to his guests, leaving them alone for five minutes while he retired to his study to attend to a small matter of business. The matter in question was tacitly assumed to be the consumption of a small glass of port, and this no one would grudge him.

My mother, who liked a glass of white wine with her dinner, now drank fruit-cup instead. Mr. Asquith recalled dining with my parents during the war. As he sipped this fruit-cup with a slightly wry and disappointed expression, my mother turned to him and explained, using an uncharacteristic slang phrase: 'You see, we've been "carted".' Quite rightly, she often had her own special pitcher of fruit-cup, which was well spiked with champagne, and from which I was also served when I came back on leave from active service.

My father, unlike my grandfather, cared little for social life in any form; he and my mother led a quiet domestic existence, enjoying that complete privacy of the home which, paradoxically enough, can only be achieved by royalty, protected as they are from the outside world. In London they dined alone together almost every night, only occasionally being obliged to entertain officially, and preferring to invite relatives to join them. They seldom accepted invitations to private dinners, and then only to a few 'great houses'. My brothers and I, when we wanted to see 'the parents', knew that we had but to telephone any morning of the week, to propose ourselves for dinner that evening, for they would seldom be otherwise engaged.

When they were alone, they would sit by the fire and read. My father, unlike my grandfather, played no card games, nor did he take kindly to the radio, beyond listening occasionally to the news. It was a long time before he could himself be persuaded to broadcast, but when at last he did so, from Sandringham, on Christmas Day, 1932, the gesture was greatly appreciated by his people. I myself fell into disfavour on this occasion for not listening to his talk. After a broadcast of my own, a few weeks later, I wrote to him contritely:

> I did appreciate your 'listening in' particularly as you thought that my playing golf instead of 'listening in' to you on Christmas Day showed great disinterestedness. That was, of course, the very last impression I meant to convey and there was *nobody* more delighted than I was that at last you took advantage of *the* invention of the century to talk to the Empire.

On these domestic occasions, when I dined with my father, we would always wear a white tie and tails and the Garter Star, though when he himself had no guests he would relax so far as to wear a dinner-jacket. In the day-time, of course, whenever I visited my father, I would have to put on a morning-coat.

As befitted a naval officer, he was a stickler for punctuality. Dinner was at 8.30 sharp and, to get to the Palace on time, I had often to effect a lightning change of costume. My former valet, Crisp, assures me that on such occasions I was able to shave, bathe and change into evening dress in as little as two and a half minutes. If this was so, it was largely due to him, for he would have everything prepared, in case, as often happened, I had left myself insufficient time, or had been for some reason delayed. I do not recall that I was ever more than a few seconds late—I would not have dared to be.

In the days before the First World War, the most rigid rules of costume prevailed, not only in the Palace but in the world which fell beneath its influence. If the King were in London, officers of the Brigade of Guards would be expected to wear a white tie and tails, even when they dined at the Guards' Club. Only if he were absent would a black tie be permissible. Before the war, if the King were in London, the officers would be expected to wear a top hat and frock- or morning-coat, whenever they went out in the streets.

Although these dress regulations have long since vanished, Guards officers are still subject to rules as strict for plain clothes as for uniform. The Adjutant may instruct the young officer where to go for his clothes, and inspect the cut and the fit of the suit, when made, before approving it. Each regiment preferred its own tailor—the Scots and Coldstream Guards, for example, patronizing Scholte, to whom I myself went for forty years. To this day it is easy to recognize a Guards officer in London, from his unvarying 'uniform' of dark lounge suit, white shirt, Guards tie, curly-brimmed bowler and tightly rolled umbrella.

My father remained always exceptionally conservative in his dress, following my grandfather's formal fashions, in his own more sober style, adhering to them with hardly a change until the end of his life, and thus always remaining in a sense a 'period' figure.

In his memoir of my father, Mr. John Gore records that he used, for fifty years, a gold collar stud bought as a midshipman during his world cruise in the *Bacchante*, and had it reinforced with a gold 'filling' when it showed signs of decay. His hair-brushes lasted him for half a century, with only one re-bristling. One day, during the London season, he looked out of his window and saw Sir Derek Keppel, his Master of the Household, entering the Palace in a bowler hat. 'You scoundrel,' he chaffed him. 'What do you mean by coming in here in that rat-catcher fashion? You never see me dressing like that in London.'

'Well, sir, you don't have to go about in buses,' Sir Derek replied.

'Buses! Nonsense!' my father exclaimed.

He was echoing here a phrase which my grandfather is said to have coined. Encountering a friend one day in the country, wearing a loose hacking-jacket, he exclaimed: 'Hello, been rat-catching?' Thereafter the name of rat-catcher was always used, as to this day, to denote such an informal riding-jacket, worn as a rule for hacking or 'cubbing', before the hunting season begins.

My father's gloves were invariably black-pointed, as his own father's had been. I never saw him in a soft collar, though he did adopt the modern turned-down collar, in place of the wing collar. His shirts were seldom striped and never coloured. His socks were always of wool, usually hand-knitted, never of silk. He continued to prefer the sideways crease in his trousers. He hardly ever wore shoes, adhering faithfully to the buttoned, cloth-topped or even elastic-sided boots of earlier days—a practical enough support for the feet for one subjected to the strain of continual standing. But his heels were a shade lower than those of my grandfather who, being short and corpulent, liked them high.

My father's overcoats were unfashionably long: a short overcoat, he used to say, is only a half-coat. He preferred a hard hat to a soft one, remarking that it was easier to lift. Once he rebuked me for not wearing a top hat on one of my trips to the Midlands, accepting only grudgingly my contention that, while all very well for official receptions, this headgear was not very suitable for visits to factories.

He preferred brown or grey suits to the more fashionable blue, once remarking that he had seen quite enough blue in the Navy. He would have felt undressed without a pin in his tie, and liked especially to wear a diamond and platinum pin, given him by his uncle, the Duke of Edinburgh, fifty years before. It was one of a large collection of pins which I inherited at his death. Since I hardly ever wear a pin in my tie, I had the tops of them mounted on the Duchess's various gold accessories, which she carries in her handbag: a jewelled horseshoe, for example, on a compact; King Edward's monogram on a case for her comb.

Few of his clothes were of any use to me at his death. Not only were they out of fashion, but they did not fit me. I did, however, take one of his Inverness capes, and a Rothesay hunting tartan suit, which he used to wear for tea after shooting: I had this altered to fit me, substituting zip-flies—which I fear would have horrified my father—for buttons. It still contains, in the pocket, a tab bearing my father's name—H.R.H. The Duke of York—and the date 1897. So it is more than sixty years old—a long enough life for a suit, in all conscience.

My father thus set few, if any, fashions. Certainly his habit of wearing his tie passed through a ring, instead of tied in a knot, was not imitated by many of his subjects. Nevertheless, out of consideration for them, he bowed on occasion to the informal trend. He wore a bowler, often a grey or a brown one, instead of a top hat, with a lounge suit instead of a morning-coat at Newmarket or Goodwood, as his father had done towards the end of his reign; and he publicly abandoned the frock-coat for the lounge suit at the opening of the Chelsea Flower Show—doubtless to the relief of innumerable country gentlemen.

An essential accessory, to the well-dressed man in the nineteenth century, was the cane or walking-stick. Doubtless it originated from the riding whip. My grandfather and father would not have dreamt of going out without carrying one of these elegant weapons, surmounted by gold or tortoiseshell knobs or handles, of which they both had large collections, while my grandmother and my mother and their contemporaries carried parasols. Gentlemen had special canes for the evening, some of them sheathing light swords for self-defence when walking home late at night.

While the rolled-up umbrella is still *de rigueur* for Guards officers and city men, the cane seems almost to have disappeared. I used to carry one until the late nineteen-twenties. Then, after a visit to America, where the cane is almost unknown, I discarded it as a bit of impedimenta which was not only unnecessary but inconvenient, for it was always getting lost or, worse still, tripping me up.

The only respect in which I followed the sartorial tastes of my father was in the materials of his country clothes. He liked bright checks in his tweeds, and so did I. In my album there are photographs of us together, thus dressed, save that I am not wearing the eight-buttoned spats that he wore over his stockings, almost up to the knees, and that the cut of my clothes is a thought more casual than his. Nor did I often wear gloves for shooting, as he invariably did.

Shooting was my father's favourite sport. He became a better shot than my grandfather, despite his modest disclaimer after a day at Hall Barn, to the late Lord Burnham: 'I can't hit a feather! But I've been at sea for a good many years and one doesn't see many pheasants there!' It was here that, at a fabulous pheasant shoot which I have described elsewhere, he later shot a thousand out of the total bag of four thousand birds.

My father was, rightly, a stern disciplinarian, as far as the use of a gun was concerned, and when he took us out shooting at Sandringham, where I bagged my first rabbit at the age of twelve, he would send us home for any breach of shooting manners or security rules.

My letters to him usually contained such a phrase as 'I hope you had good sport' or 'I am sorry you had bad sport' at Bolton, or Wynyard, or West Dean, or Studley Royal, or one of the other stately homes where he shot each year. But my spelling was not always all it should have been. 'I am glad to hear,' I once wrote in 1908, 'you have had fine weather, but you told me at Abergeldie that it was not a good year for partrages.' An alternative spelling I favoured, at that age, was 'partrige'. My father would always send me his game cards; and I, if I was shooting away from home, would send him mine.

But there came a time when he began to discourage my shooting. One day in 1912, from H.M.S. *Medina*, close to Suez, on his way back from India, he dashed off a letter to me, waiving his customary prefix of 'My dearest David' (once he had written absent-mindedly 'My dearest Papa'), and coming straight to the point:

> Judging from your letters and from the number of days you have been out shooting, there can't be much game left at Sandringham, I should think. It also seems a mistake to shoot the coverts three times over, I never do that unless a few more cocks have to be killed. I can't understand Bland wishing you to do so. You seem to be having too much shooting and not enough riding or hunting. I can't understand why you did not hunt when Sir C. Fitzwilliam came expressly for that, and Bertie and Harry went out, what on earth were you doing? You must learn to ride and hunt properly and you have had such good chances this winter at Sandringham. I must say I am disappointed.

This new grievance became a recurrent theme in his letters:

> In your position, it is absolutely necessary that you should ride well as you will continually have to do so at parades, reviews, etc., and so the sooner you make up your mind to it the better. The English people like riding and it would make you very unpopular if you couldn't do so. If you can't ride, you know, I am afraid people will call you a duffer.

For all my father's lectures, I could ride and indeed took to fox-hunting at Oxford, with the University Draghounds and the neighbouring packs. But I had been brought up in a shooting rather than a hunting country, at Sandringham, and the unique chance of enjoying the run of its famous coverts that season, during my father's absence in India, should not be wasted, in my view, for the sake of a run with the local foxhounds. My father himself liked to ride, hacking in Rotten Row and in the Great Park at Windsor. But he never hunted or jumped fences.

As it happened, I came to enjoy hunting more and more, at first to my father's satisfaction:

> Delighted [he was writing some two years later] that you enjoyed and got on so well on Monday, your first day's hunting. Cadogan said you went very well. . . . Now that you have confidence in yourself and your horse, I know you will like it. I am glad you are going to hunt again next week and have your last day on Thursday, hope it will be a good one and we shall expect you here at about 7.30, of course come in your hunting clothes unless you are wet, when you can change in the train.

There is an ironical twist in the fact that, ten years later, my father's letters became equally forcible in their insistence that I should, in the interests of my safety, give up riding in point-to-point races, a matter in which, as I have recorded elsewhere, I eventually—and reluctantly—bowed to his wishes. Thenceforward I virtually gave up riding, and devoted more of my time to that 'tiresome golf', as my father called it, and later on to gardening.

It was not always easy to please my father. Even when I took to hunting, in the first place, he was not wholly content with me. He wrote to me at Oxford:

> You certainly have been doing a great deal, hunting two days, out with the beagles twice, golf and shooting one day, besides all your work, which seems a good deal for one week. I only hope you are not overdoing it in the way of exercise.

'Take less exercise' was one of his perennial injunctions. 'I hope,' he would say, 'you will not overdo it at squash rackets or in taking too much exercise.'

Another was, 'Eat more. . . . It all depends now in the next two or three years whether you develop into a strong healthy man or remain a sort of puny half-grown boy.' My thinness and lightness of weight were a constant source of worry to him—as, indeed, they are to my wife, perhaps the sole preoccupation she has in common with King George V. Rather as he kept a game book, he kept also a weighing book, in which the family weights were recorded at intervals.

> I see by the weighing book here that on December 22, 1910, you weighed 7 st. 13 lbs., and when I weighed you at Balmoral you were 7 st. 8 lbs., so instead of increasing you have lost 5 lbs. in nearly three years, that is certainly not as it should be.

To this I replied:

> I was weighed this morning and reached 8 stones. . . . I will let you know my weight each week when I write.

But my father was always quick to assure me that these various injunctions were 'for my own good'. And so, I am convinced, they were. 'I want you to treat me,' he wrote, 'as your best friend. . . . My great wish is that you should be happy and be fitted for the position that you will some day occupy in this country.' And if ever I pleased him, he was generous enough to say so. It was gratifying at the age of thirteen to receive an epistle from the moors at Bolton Abbey, which said: 'I must compliment you on your manners and general behaviour. Everyone was very pleased with you at Cowes.'

CHAPTER VII

LOCOMOTION

Not long ago, the Duchess and I were crossing in the train-ferry boat from West Palm Beach to Havana. We fell into conversation with an elderly American couple, who were travelling with three young grandchildren. These children, who had come to stay with their grandparents for the Easter holidays, were in a state of some excitement. It was the first time they had ever travelled aboard a steamship. Moreover, a few days before, they had enjoyed an experience as memorable. They had travelled for the first time on a train. With their parents they had indeed been travelling since they were out of their cradles—but always, being children of this age, by car or by aeroplane, vehicles of transport which had no mysteries for them.

So do times change. In my childhood it was the train and the steamship that we took for granted, the car and the aeroplane that became a source of excitement later. Trains took us in our seasonal peregrinations to and from Windsor, Sandringham and Balmoral, while to Osborne, in the Isle of Wight, we crossed the Solent in a small steamer from Portsmouth. But they provided a diversion none the less.

In our journeys to Aberdeen, for Balmoral, it was diverting to sleep on the train. We travelled in a 'bed-carriage', in a berth still precisely like that designed for Queen Adelaide, the wife of King William IV. It stretched not along but across the seats, which were linked for the purpose by a close-fitting stool with an upholstered cushion. Our journeys to Wolferton, for Sandringham, were an enjoyable picnic. There were no dining-cars on this route in those days, so we took a well-stocked luncheon-basket, and when the train stopped at a suitable station, were regaled with coffee from a trolley on the platform. On returning from Sandringham, each guest or member of the Household would be supplied with his own luncheon-basket, packed in the royal kitchen. They would be left on the train at St. Pancras Station, cleaned and washed up by the Great Eastern Railway, and returned to Marlborough House or later to Buckingham Palace, when my grandfather became King.

To keep us warm in the winter, there would be foot-warmers, covered with carpeting and filled with boiling water. Queen Victoria had a heated compartment of her own as early as the eighteen-forties. It was fitted with a small hot-water boiler beneath the floor. She had first travelled on a train from Slough to London in 1842, taking twenty-five minutes over the journey—which is no faster today—and arriving at Paddington amid, as the Press put it, 'deafening demonstrations of loyalty and affection'. She returned by the same means a week later, this time taking with her my future grandfather, the baby Prince of Wales.

My great-grandmother would never, until the end of her days, eat a meal on a train. Before setting out for Balmoral, she would dine early at Windsor, and a kind of high-tea-supper would be served to her on the journey, at Banbury Station. She had other idiosyncrasies. Her royal saloon, built in 1869, was lit by oil and candle lamps, with delicate lace shades. At a later date the railway company, keeping abreast of the times, fitted it with gas lamps. But the Queen was not amused, and ordered their instant removal. When electric light came in, the company installed it, but left the original fittings unchanged in appearance. This did not fool my great-grandmother, who insisted that in her own carriage the oil and candle lamps should be retained as before.

Her orders, on these occasions, were transmitted through the 'coarse mouthpiece'—as Mr. G. P. Neale, the operating superintendent called it—of John Brown who, as the Queen's personal attendant, had a compartment of his own in the royal saloon. On one occasion, as Mr. Neale recalls in his memoirs, he was ordered to stop the train at Wigan. When he had done so, John Brown explained: 'The Queen says the carriage was shaking like the devil.'

She refused to travel at more than fifty miles an hour. Thus her train journeys, preceded always by a pilot engine to clear the line, were slow affairs. Those of the Shah of Persia, when he visited England, were slower still, since he considered that twenty miles an hour was quite fast enough.

King Edward, however, was all for speed, provided it was compatible with safety. When a new royal train was built for him, he asked that in style and decoration it should resemble, as nearly as possible, the Royal Yacht. It was to this train that bathrooms were added for my mother and father, who had to live on it for days at a time while touring the country during the First World War.

At home we still drove in horse-drawn carriages—wagonettes as a rule, brakes, dog-carts and pony-carriages. My grandfather, I remember, had a special pony-carriage like a Victoria, from which for a time he used to shoot. He had injured his leg, tripping over a rabbit hole in Windsor Great Park, and shot standing up in it, having taken the wise precaution of unharnessing the pony beforehand.

The perfection of the 'safety bicycle', towards the turn of the century, brought us, as children, a welcome new lease of freedom. Previously, if we wanted to go farther afield than the grounds of Windsor or Sandringham, we had been limited by the necessity of asking, through a nurse or a tutor, for a carriage and a coachman from the royal stables, with all the harnessing and grooming and general fuss which such an operation involved. Then my grandfather gave me my first bicycle, and my life was transformed. My brothers and I were soon living on bicycles. We could thus get away on our own, riding races and going for ten-mile rides along the public roads which were still, in those days, free from motor traffic or, indeed, from any serious volume of traffic at all. We thus began to see something of the world outside the gardens and grounds of the places where we lived.

The bicycles we rode were a distinct improvement on the insecure 'penny-farthings' of a previous generation. When these became fashionable, my great-uncle, the Duke of Connaught, took to riding one. Uncle Arthur was a charming man and a distinguished soldier, but a somewhat clumsy fellow in his movements. He was always tripping and falling when he walked, and his seat on a horse was none too secure. Nevertheless, he took to bicycling with relish.

One day, having promised to present prizes to the gentlemen cadets at a sports meeting at the Royal Military College at Sandhurst, he insisted on riding over from his house at Bagshot, on his penny-farthing bicycle, while some of his family, my father included, and his suite accompanied him on theirs. On entering the college grounds, the Duke saw all the cadets drawn up to welcome him. Always punctilious and polite in his manners, he raised his hat, lifting a hand from the handle-bars to do so. It was a disastrous gesture. Unable to balance himself with one hand on his high and precarious velocipede, he fell ignominiously to the ground in front of all the cadets, with the bicycle on top of him.

The last time I rode a bicycle was in Nassau, when I was Governor of the Bahamas during the war. There was a shortage of gasoline in the islands, and we started a campaign to dissuade the inhabitants from using their cars for private purposes. To set an example, I took to bicycling in the late afternoon from Government House to our cabaña down on the beach for a swim. In a further effort to make the Bahamians bicycle-conscious, an official with a sense of public relations produced a tandem—a 'bicycle made for two'—and suggested that the Duchess and I should be photographed riding it together. We got on to the bicycle, but failed after a short run to keep our balance, and fell to the ground as Uncle Arthur had done. But we had not so far to fall.

Living in France, a land of bicycles, it is hard to escape all the fuss and excitement over the annual 'Tour de France', a national bicycle race which lasts for three weeks during the month of July. If one is planning a motor trip in France at that time, it is imperative to obtain the official schedule of the race, for which long stretches of the *routes nationales* are closed to all other traffic save the competitors. They start from Paris and race up and down mountains and through the flatter country, finishing in the capital, where they started.

The physical strain on the riders is prodigious, as may be imagined, and they take terrible spills, often involving broken heads and limbs. Fortunately, only very rarely are the accidents fatal. The route into Paris is changed each year, to give the neighbouring small towns, villages and suburbs a chance to view the survivors pedalling away to the finish. They passed within a quarter of a mile from the Mill one year, and we took our week-end guests to watch this phenomenal test of endurance.

Meanwhile—to revert to my boyhood—motor-cars were coming in. My grandfather himself travelled in a British-built Bersey Electric cab, all the way from Marlborough House to Buckingham Palace and back, as early as 1897. His first drive in a car had been in the previous year when he attended a demonstration of a Daimler carriage at the Imperial Institute, South Kensington. Mr. Evelyn Ellis drove him through the gallery of the Institute and then actually out into the open, 'executing', according to *The Autocar*, 'some most skilful manœuvres in stopping, starting and generally handling the vehicle. The Prince expressed himself as highly pleased . . . giving vent to the hope, however, that automobiles would not entirely supersede horses'. It was a hope in which he was destined to be disappointed.

Within a few years, he himself owned a motor-car, a 12 h.p. Daimler, which still survives as a vintage specimen. The purchase was arranged by Mr. Oliver Stanton, an American who acted as consultant to the Daimler firm, and who gave my grandfather his first driving lessons at Sandringham. Later he bought a 22 h.p. model, of which we read: 'The rear seats are raised about five inches higher than the level of the front seat, so that His Majesty will be able to get an uninterrupted view of the road.' The King showed an intelligent interest in the mechanism of his cars, examining every part with care and being quoted in the Press as an example to 'other notable and wealthy automobilists', who regarded their cars simply as a convenient means of locomotion.

It was King Edward's friend, John Montagu of Beaulieu, who had first aroused his serious interest in motoring, using it indeed as a means of popularizing this 'new-fangled invention', until it became taken for granted as an element in the national life. Mr. Montagu had taken my grandfather on his first long drive over the public roads through the New Forest from Highcliff Castle, where he was staying at the time. The car was an open 12 h.p. Daimler, its back wheels twice as large as its front. It had no windshield, its front seats were upright and uncomfortable, and there was only just room for the two ladies he had invited, who sat perched in the back. When the car reached forty miles an hour, they had to cling on to their hats. 'The Prince, enjoying the unwonted speed,' as Mr. Montagu later recorded, 'chaffed, in his cheery way, his fair companions and made the true remark that motoring would force ladies to adopt some special form of head-dress.' Within a few years they were indeed wearing hats tied on to their heads with motoring veils, together with dust-coats and goggles to protect them from the elements.

Visiting Beaulieu a few years later, the King was held up at the Lymington Toll Bridge, while driving with Mr. Montagu. In *The Motoring Montagus*, his son records the dialogue which followed between Montagu and the old toll-keeper:

> 'Hurry up and open the gate. Can't you see His Majesty the King is with me?'
>
> 'I know them Kings. One of 'em slipped past me only this morning. Pay your sixpence first and then you can wait until I've let this donkey-cart through.'
>
> 'But it's the King!' John Montagu protested.
>
> 'King or no king, who was it who went through my gate without paying this morning?'

I well remember my first ride in a 'horseless carriage'—as motor-cars were then called—at the turn of the century. It was in the fall of 1902, and the occasion was the planting of an avenue of trees to commemorate my grandfather's Coronation in the summer of that year. My father was not slow to follow King Edward's pioneer spirit, in popularizing the vehicles of the new gasoline age but, being of a more cautious nature, he first acquired an electric car, run on batteries and steered with a handle bar, as opposed to the conventional steering wheel.

From York Cottage we sallied forth to the rendezvous for the tree-planting ceremony, some two miles away. I forget who actually drove the electric car, but I do

My father, then Prince of Wales. At the time no gentleman would wear this kind of lounge-suit in London. Not until nearly twenty-five years later did he publicly abandon wearing a frock-coat on formal occasions in London

My father as Duke of York in 1893, wearing a morning-coat with tweedy trousers, as was the fashion

Bertie, George and I listening to the Proclamation of King George V in 1910

Myself at the age of ten, wearing sailor's uniform, at that time traditional wear for boys

In 1911, dressed in the full costume of a Knight of the Garter which I wore at my father's Coronation later that year

On a visit to France in 1912

With Dr. W. G. Grace, the famous cricketer of the period. Although still in my late teens, I was already taking an interest in clothes

With my mother, Bertie and Mary in Scotland in 1913

remember that his handle-bar moustache was almost as long as the implement with which he steered us at the modest speed of twenty m.p.h. to join the distinguished company. This, on my grandfather's invitation, included the Kaiser.

It was afterwards recorded of me in *The Car*: 'Prince Edward is not yet an automobilist in that he owns his own car, but it is generally understood that he enjoys being on an automobile, and is immensely delighted with the mode of progress.'

The Kaiser also took up motoring with enthusiasm. When my grandfather paid an official visit to Potsdam some years later, the lamps on the German Imperial car, put at his disposal, had been embossed with the English royal crown. When my father visited Potsdam in the year preceding the outbreak of the First World War, he wrote to me: 'We rarely went in carriages, always in motors and William likes going very fast, even in the town.'

My next recollection of motoring is of my return for the holidays from the Royal Naval College at Osborne a few years later. My mother asked me how I would like to spend the afternoon. I said I would like to ride in a taxi, a vehicle which I had seen advertised in the Press and which was beginning to grow popular. So a taxi was whistled up to Marlborough House, a rattling contraption with a polished brass lamp and accoutrements, hard leather seats and a rubber bulb horn, and with Finch, our personal servant, I took my first taxi-drive around London.

In those days the custom, in summoning a vehicle, was to blow one blast for a four-wheeler, two for a hansom and now three for a taxi. But within a few years taxis had become so numerous that this practice was reversed, and the rule became one blast for a taxi, two for a hansom and three for the dying four-wheeler.

Taxis were known for many years as 'mechanical Clarences', after the four-wheeled closed carriage which King William IV had used as Duke of Clarence. At this time they were mostly imported from Paris, where they were reputed to 'have the attraction of great speed'. There was considerable debate as to whether they should be named taxis, motor-cabs, taxi-cabs, or taximeter cabs; the simpler name 'taxi' eventually stuck. Their drivers were traditionally civil, and in 1910 decided at a meeting not to smoke without the passenger's permission.

King Edward, in these early days of motoring, used to express concern as to the threat to the British motor industry of foreign competition, even declaring on one occasion that he would never have a car of foreign manufacture. He did indeed remain faithful to the British-built Daimler; but only after his fashion. A few years later he was buying a German Mercedes, a make of car to which he had doubtless taken a fancy during his visits to Marienbad. There is a story that the Mercedes agent there, anxious to advertise the superiority of his own car, interfered with the gears of the royal Daimler, so that it stuck on a hill, obliging the King to walk up. A Daimler expert was immediately and peremptorily summoned from England—and exposed his rival's sabotage.

But this did not seem to deter King Edward who bought, in succession, three Mercedes. Diplomatic in his instincts, and doubtless anxious to strike a balance of power between Germany and France, he also bought a Renault landaulette, which was used by Queen Alexandra during her widowhood and was inherited by my father at her death. But these vehicles were largely for private journeys; the Daimler remained the official royal car. And so it is today.

My father remained staunchly loyal to Daimlers. One of them was an open shooting-brake—roomy enough to accommodate stalkers, ghillies or gamekeepers, besides himself, to say nothing of bird dogs—the forerunner of the modern station wagon. At Balmoral he would sometimes stop to shoot a stag from it. Five years before his death, in October 1930, my father chose the moment of the world slump, with its threat of unemployment, to place an order for five new cars—more than any King had ever ordered before—for delivery in the following spring, and thus kept the Daimler works employed throughout a long workless winter.

The first car I owned, while I was still at Oxford, was also a Daimler. Undergraduates were not allowed motor-cars in my time, firstly to prevent traffic jams in the narrow streets, and secondly as a sacrifice on the altar of democracy. It would have led to a lot of trouble and jealousy, had only those who could afford the luxury owned cars. So we undergraduates had to ride bicycles, fastening clips to our trousers, skidding and colliding with one another on the muddy greasy streets.

However, if we were going out of Oxford to hunt or visit friends in the neighbourhood, we were allowed to hire cars. Then, in the summer of 1913 I wrote to my father:

> I have thought that it would be much less expensive if I got one now, though of course I would not do so without your permission.

The permission was reluctantly granted and a 39 h.p. touring model Daimler, painted blue and upholstered in blue leather, was duly delivered. I kept it at the Morris Garage, where it was housed and serviced by the present Lord Nuffield.

I was, of course, careful never to use this car for my university activities, and stuck to my bicycle for going to lectures. But it was on other occasions a great boon to my friends, who had no cars, and soon I was taking it abroad on my vacations. At the age of nineteen I was naturally often exceeding the speed limit, and a report about me in *The Times*, a newspaper which my father read daily from cover to cover, to the effect that 'He drove his motor-car with enthusiastic speed', did not escape the paternal eye. My father never learnt to drive himself, and he had already written to me:

> I must beg of you not to drive fast and to be most careful when you are driving, it makes both Mama and me most anxious, as any little mistake and the accident occurs. I must confess I do not approve of your driving a motor and have always said so. But as you say it gives you great pleasure, I am willing to let you do so, providing you will promise not to drive fast and to be most careful while you are in Germany. It is impossible for you to drive as well as an expert who does it every day of his life and you must remember your position and who you are, and that the slightest accident that you might have would be exaggerated and in every paper in Europe. I shall say no more as you know my views.

As a matter of fact this Oxford car of mine was the last Daimler I owned until I inherited my father's 'stable' of them at his death. For a time after the war I had a Rolls-

Royce, then a Bentley, and one or two Hillmans. Later I took to Buicks, which were, in deference to the Empire, Canadian- and not American-made. Since my Abdication, I have usually had American cars.

Always ready to try anything new, I was persuaded by the inventor to acquire, during the nineteen-twenties, an experimental Burney Streamline car, designed by a retired naval officer, Sir Charles Dennistoun Burney, M.P., who had, more successfully, invented the paravane for mine-sweeping, and had been concerned in the design of the airship R.100. This car had its engine at the back, instead of the front—an arrangement which, before the days of heating in cars, made it uncomfortably chilly.

My Burney was not a good climber of hills, maybe because its engine was too weak, and, to the disgust of my driver, had an inconvenient habit of stalling. I remember an afternoon when I was driving to Windsor, and the car stopped suddenly in the midst of the traffic on the outskirts of London. Its curious appearance attracted considerable attention, especially when the crowd saw that I was inside it. Since it obstinately refused to start up again, I was obliged to send my driver to telephone for one of my other cars before I could continue my journey. This Burney car, I believe, now languishes in a garage in North London, where together with one of my old Buicks, it is shown off to an occasional visitor as the Prince of Wales's car.

I have never been very much interested in cars as such, and nowadays rarely drive myself. I spend the time more profitably in the back seat, doing my 'home-work', and have a special reading-lamp installed in my cars for use after dark.

CHAPTER VIII

TRAVEL

My father did not care for travelling. He used to say that he had had his fill of it as a young man in the Navy, when he spent a number of years abroad on foreign naval stations. All he wanted as he grew older was to stay at home. He even disapproved of my going away for week-ends from London, a practice in which he never indulged himself.

On his first world cruise, as a midshipman in the *Bacchante*, the flagship of the 'Flying Squadron', he and his brother the Duke of Clarence were accompanied by Dr. John N. Dalton, that lifelong mentor and friend of his, who afterwards became a Canon of St. George's Chapel, Windsor. I have many memories of the old Canon, but few of his son, Hugh, who was later destined to become a Socialist Chancellor of the Exchequer. Because of these left-wing political views, which he developed at an early age, Hugh Dalton was no favourite of my father who, once inviting the Canon to Sunday luncheon at Frogmore, added with jocular severity: 'But don't bring that anarchist son of yours with you!'

It was the Canon's task to record my father's tours, for the benefit of posterity.

Unlike my father, I myself have never tired of travelling. I now love, it is true, to stay quietly at our two homes in France, endeavouring to cultivate my garden, but the pleasures of this become all the keener by contrast with the times I still spend travelling in America and elsewhere. When, after the First World War, I began my world tours aboard the battle cruisers *Renown* and *Repulse*, I had no such official scribe as the Canon to record my progress. It was amply and more readably recorded by the Press of the world. But I was, on the second of my cruises, well served by an unofficial scribe, my second cousin Lord Louis Mountbatten—well known as Dickie—who wrote, as we proceeded, a day-to-day diary 'of the Staff, by the Staff, for the Staff', which he describes as 'frankly frivolous and not official in any sense'. It stands out today in lively contrast to the ponderous chronicle of the late lamented Canon Dalton.

Lord Mountbatten of Burma, as he now is, owes his distinguished Naval career, in an indirect sense, to my father. For, when the personnel of the Navy was reduced in 1922, Dickie, as an officer, with, after his marriage, substantial alternative means of support, was threatened with the 'axe'. Hearing of this and of the young officer's despair at the threat to a career which had been his own father's, and on which he had set his heart from boyhood, King George expressed a wish that he should be permitted to remain in the Navy. And so the country gained a great sailor. Dickie Mountbatten had about him all the breeziness of humour which the sea seems to bring out in those who serve her, and his diary, which I have lately been re-reading, brings back to me many of the lighter incidents of those memorable trips.

Not the least of these, since clothes make the prince, were concerned with matters of costume—the day-by-day problem of what to wear, and when to wear it. I had to change my clothes as often, and as quickly, as any actor on the stage—from naval into military and from full-dress into undress uniform, from 'blues' into 'whites', from golfing tweeds into top hats and morning-coats—what a garden party invitation in the Canadian West defined as: 'Plug-hat and Streamline Morning'. Sometimes I was caught between changes, as when, nearing Brisbane on the train, I was surprised by the crowds, and appeared waving to them clad only in breeches, boots and spurs, and an open shirt with a pair of Brigade of Guards braces.

My travelling wardrobe was, of course, immense. I carried some forty tin trunks, each numbered and with its contents listed in a series of inventory notebooks. But I seldom set eyes on these. All I saw were the two large hanging trunks set up in my cabin, or in my sleeping-compartment, or my bedroom ashore, packed in advance to contain all I would require to wear for the next three days. My valet, Jack Crisp, whose task it was thus to plan my costume ahead, much as a general plans an operation, remembers only one occasion on which he slipped up in his plans. On laying out my clothes for a change into field service uniform, he found that he had left me without a khaki tie, and made me one on the spot. It was one of the best ties I ever had.

His planning operations covered also the matter of getting my dirty linen washed. H.M.S. *Renown* lacked the amenity of a laundry; washing was done ashore in the various places we visited. Thus Jack had to see that I was equipped with enough shirts and underclothes to last me for fourteen days at sea, if need be. He had to become an expert, too, on the intricate accessories of naval and military dress.

Accidents would occur, none the less. Shoulder straps would be missing, making it impossible to wear aiguillettes; hats would mysteriously vanish; we would be photographed wearing white socks instead of black ones. Once the Surgeon Commander's mess jacket was forgotten, and he had to appear at an official dinner wearing a dinner-jacket and gold lace trousers, 'a combination', as Dickie's dairy recalls, 'which had never been dreamt of, even in the most heated of the many Staff discussions re dress'.

One such misadventure, at Melbourne, he justly blames on myself.

> It rained in torrents during the early part of the morning, and H.R.H. seized on the opportunity to abolish top hats and carriages for the races. The result of this was that he was caught in his own trap, for when he came to dress, his Christy Stiff was nowhere to be found, so that he had to go in a squash hat, and the rest of the Staff went in bowlers. The hat was found half an hour later in the A.D.C.'s waste-paper-basket and sent on to the racecourse. The Captain and Ship's officers had a surprise as they had come in tall hats and according to themselves, felt fools, even if they did not look it.

On another occasion, it was the Prime Minister of Australia, 'Billy' Hughes, who was—or so I thought—at fault. He came to lunch on a Sunday at Government

House, wearing riding-kit but only a single spur. Since we all liked to tease Mr. Hughes, I pointed out to him that he had left a spur behind. But his disarming reply was that he always dressed this way. He had no such reply ready when, at a garden party, his small daughter looked searchingly up at him and declared: 'Daddy, you know that's not your hat.'

One day we went down a gold mine with him, all rigged out in brown overalls. The Prime Minister presented a curious spectacle, since he had neglected to tuck his morning-coat inside his overalls, and its tails hung outside them looking distinctly comic, and, in the end, becoming distinctly dirty.

Dickie himself slipped up in the West Indies, when he discovered, as the ship was about to sail, that some items of his uniform had been left behind on the island of Antigua. We were already under way when a native sailing boat drew up alongside the *Renown* with a Negro standing in the bows. He had a pair of white trousers in one hand and a tunic in the other, and was signalling in semaphore: 'Have suit of clothes for you.' To Dickie's relief, they were his.

One evening at sea the most sedate of my Equerries, Lord Claud Hamilton, lost the lower part of his uniform. But this, I regret to say, was a deliberate operation, carried out after a boisterous evening in the gun-room with myself sitting disrespectfully on His Lordship's head while Dickie and others removed his nether garments. 'Nevertheless,' the Staff diary records, 'he behaved as a soldier should and as he pattered past the sentry, orderly and the two messengers, in his bare legs, he found time for a pleasant word with each of them.'

Our high spirits led us often into such pranks, of which poor Lord Claud and my Private Secretary, Sir Godfrey Thomas, were good-tempered victims. They even kept their tempers when, on returning late one night from a dance my cousin and I put them down on the slate to be called at 5 a.m., and thus deprived them of their precious morning beauty sleep.

Our preoccupation with uniforms was immortalized in a verse of a rhymed alphabet composed by one of the Staff.

U is the Uniform worn by the Staff
Naval cocked hats—how the crowds used to chaff:
Fluttering seagulls, crimson and white,
Gold lace and garters, a wonderful sight.
(If you liked a good argument, far the best way
Was to start a discussion on rig of the day.)

One such discussion arose, I remember, during my visit to Japan. The Japanese Crown Prince had issued invitations to myself and my staff to a garden party, at the Imperial Palace, intimating that civilian frock-coats would be worn, as was customary at the Japanese Court, and moreover that gentlemen wearing morning-coats would not be admitted. The Japanese officials had to be informed that we had brought no such garment. Finally the difficulty was solved by our appearance in undress uniform, which included the naval or military frock-coat. As for the civilian members of my staff, they kept their overcoats on throughout the garden party.

Throughout these various tours, my father, a man who, like my grandfather, had strict notions on the subject of uniforms, watched the Press photographs of me keenly and was quick to detect any errors in costume. Thus he wrote to me in New Zealand:

> From various photographs of you which have appeared in the papers I see that you wear turned-down collars in white uniform, with a collar and black tie. I wonder whose idea that was, as anything more unsmart I never saw; I have worn tunics for 20 years in white, which was very smart.

In this, as in most such niceties of uniform, my father was perfectly correct. The shirt, collar and tie, worn with a white jacket, had been introduced by the Admiralty, supposedly in the interests of comfort, as an optional alternative to the white tunic buttoning high at the neck. It turned out in fact to be far less comfortable, involving as it did, in hot weather, an extra layer of clothing. After trying this for a while, my Staff and I came greatly to prefer the old tunic, for it could be worn with only an undershirt beneath it, and when we relaxed, in the tropics, could be loosened at the neck, thus affording us some relief. So, on my tour of India the following year, the innovation of the collar and tie was abandoned, and my father was justifiably satisfied.

This letter contained a second rebuke:

> I think you ought to censor Brookes' photos that he sends to the papers, as you and Dick in a swimming-bath together is hardly dignified, though comfortable in a hot climate, you might as well be photographed *naked* no doubt it would please the public.

In this, in such heat, it was harder to satisfy him. To India he wrote to me, in the following year:

> I have just seen in the papers different pictures of you in India, and . . . I am surprised to see that you and your Staff are wearing blue overalls with your white tunics. A most extraordinarily ugly uniform. I wonder when the order was given, as white overalls have always been worn with white tunics by the Army in India. The regulations ought never to have been altered without my approval. I will find out from the C.-in-C. when these orders were given, as I consider that the white uniform has been entirely ruined, besides being very uncomfortable in that weather.

This was a case of conflict between Army and Navy traditions. The Navy, in hot climates, often wore a blue coat with white trousers, but never a white coat with blue ones. I myself preferred the blue overalls, which were of a softer material, hence more comfortable, despite my father, than the stiff drill overalls—and moreover showed the dirt less at the foot. But such a reversal of tradition was anathema to the King, and my Staff and I were obliged to give up the practice. It continued to be followed, nevertheless, by certain units of the Army in India, greatly to the satisfaction and comfort of Sir John Aird, later my Equerry, who was on the staff of the Governor of Bombay, and who stuck to blue overalls throughout his service there.

From India originated two items of costume, which were destined to become widely popular in Britain. One was suède shoes and ankle-boots, usually with rope soles, which in the Second World War were to become the favourite footgear of the Desert forces. I started to wear them in the 'twenties, and remember doing so on a visit to America in 1924. I noticed, however, that my American friends were looking down at my feet with some embarrassment. Finally someone explained to me that the wearing of these shoes in America was regarded as effeminate, to say the least of it. I hastily explained that in England they carried no such stigma; but tactfully forebore from wearing them again.

Another importation from India was jodhpurs, that handy substitute for breeches which Indians wear, and whose name is derived from the State of Jodhpur. They provide the answer for all who like to ride and who lack the time and the patience to drag on, and moreover to shine, those leather riding-boots which, admittedly, look so much smarter. Jodhpurs, however, date much further back than my time in India.

The late Lord Rossmore, a friend of my grandfather's, tells an amusing story concerning them. He had two pairs of jodhpurs made, with buckskin legs and cloth tops, one in black and the other in brown. Once, while shooting at Elveden, he was wearing the black pair, which caught King Edward's eye. His Majesty remarked to him, rolling his r's in characteristic fashion:

'I am glad to see, R-rossmore, that you Irish landlords are becoming more provident.'

'Why, sir?'

'Because I see that you are using up your old evening trousers to make shooting leggings.'

Years afterwards, on meeting him at Punchestown races, the King remembered the incident and inquired of him:

'Well, R-rossmore, how are the evening tr-rousers?'

When in East Africa I designed a special type of safari shorts. These were made of thick khaki drill, which could be worn long, in the bush, to protect the knees from long grasses and thorny undergrowth, or could be buttoned up above the knee for the sake of coolness on the march in more open country.

On this, as on all my tours, we virtually lived on trains, and many of our public functions took place on station platforms. I remember that at one of these on a train trip from Melbourne, Colonel Grigg, my military Secretary afterwards Lord Altrincham, became indignant at an elderly porter who was trying, not very successfully, to control the crowd:

"'Look,' exclaimed the colonel, 'he is such an old dug-out that he still has Queen Victoria's monogram on his cap!'

It was politely pointed out to him that the 'V.R.' in this case stood for Victorian Railways—for we were in the State of Victoria.

In the matter of train accommodation in Australia, there was a healthy rivalry between the railways of the east and the west. It was in Western Australia that we had the unfortunate derailment which I have described elsewhere. After it, one of the newspaper correspondents sent a reassuring telegram to his paper, from every station, each ending with the words: 'Royal train still on rails.'

In East Africa, on the royal train, I once went down with a bad bout of malaria. At the height of my fever, I asked my Equerry, Jack Aird, to call the doctor. But he explained to me that this was a train without connexions between the coaches and that the doctor was having his dinner in a separate car towards the front. 'Stop the train then,' I told him, 'I think I'm going to die.'

This gave Jack an opportunity for which, as he afterwards confessed, he had been waiting all his life. At last he had reason to pull the communication cord, without fear of a fine. He did so. But nothing happened: the train went on. Clearly the cord was not working. Then he looked out of the window, and saw that the line was on a curve, so that the rear of the train was easily visible from the engine. Being a soldier and a man of resource, he took a sheet from his bunk and flapped it out of the window, flying, as it were—also for the first time in his life—the white flag. The driver saw it and stopped the train, the doctor walked along the track, reassured me as to my condition, and we resumed our journey.

The most antiquated of all the trains I remember was in Tasmania, where there is a narrow-gauge line. The train in question had been fitted up comfortably enough, but as Dickie Mountbatten, perhaps a little unkindly, put it, 'might almost have been Stephenson's first effort'. The engine driver, however, was determined to show its paces, and though he had been warned to go slowly, set off at high speed to make up time after an unforeseen delay.

There was a speed indicator in the royal car, and I noticed that this registered only eleven—though it was clear that we were travelling a lot faster than eleven miles an hour. Playing around with the indicator, I pulled a little handle beside it, in case that might give the true speed. But the train immediately stopped. I had applied the vacuum brakes. It was all for the best, as the engine driver was instructed not to make up time, and we proceeded thenceforward at a safer and more leisurely rate.

Other blunders of mine on these tours were often of a social, hence a more awkward nature. There was the occasion in New Zealand when I was believed, through no fault of my own, to have knighted the wrong man.

But he was afterwards found, to the relief of all, to be the right one after all. Then there was the ball in Fiji at which I caused some consternation at Government House by choosing, as one of my first partners, the lady typist to the chief Indian agitator in the island.

A more embarrassing incident occurred at a reception in Melbourne, when the Prime Minister waved a hand towards the end of the room and said to me: 'That is my son.' Seeing two men standing there, I singled out the one in evening dress, and shook hands with him. He turned out to be a waiter.

The boot was on the other foot when, at a place near Kalgoorlie, the assembled schoolchildren lustily cheered the upstanding and fully uniformed State Marshal under the impression that he was myself, who was in civilian clothes. Another time, at an Australian dinner party, my charming neighbour and I were drawing pigs on the menu with our eyes shut, as a change from conversation. When my turn came, I turned to my hostess and found myself saying: 'I will look at you and get an inspiration.' The pig was far from being a good one.

In Australia there used to be dances, night after night, and I am astonished when I now think of the youthful energy of which we all seemed capable. The crowds at some of these dances were enormous. I remember an evening at the Town Hall in Melbourne, where dancing became almost impossible on account of the crowd in the ballroom, watching the dancers, and I was obliged to withdraw. The Master of Ceremonies then rose and asked all non-dancers to leave the ballroom to make more room. Thereupon all the non-dancers immediately began to dance, making the congestion worse than before.

We had some boisterous evenings in Melbourne. Once at Government House, when we were dancing to the music of a pianola, the Captain of the *Renown* brought in a pram, which belonged to the Governor's cook, put me into it and wheeled me at a break-neck speed down the ballroom, turning so sharply at the end that he spilled me out and damaged the pram considerably. The cushions fell out of it, and in a moment a rugger scrum formed around them. An impromptu game began, which continued until most of the stuffing was torn out of the cushions, flying around in the air and giving the room a distinctly debauched appearance. Only on Sundays—and after midnight on Saturdays—were there no dances. I remember a Sunday when we played ludo after dinner instead, to the music of pianola and gramophone, but when midnight struck and Monday dawned, we had a dance or two before going to bed.

These tours were an education for me. They showed me new sights, brought me in touch with new peoples, and gave me new experiences of every sort and kind. There was one experience in Japan that I missed and today I regard it as a fortunate escape. At the time however I wrote to my father:

> My chief disappointment is not being able to get *tattooed* in Japan; but it seems that it's been made illegal, though I can't think why. Still, under these conditions, I've left it severely alone!!

CHAPTER IX

NINETEEN-TWENTIES

Apart from some experience of the world, these travels brought me another enduring blessing. They brought me friends—friends, for the most part, among the members of my staff, with whom I lived and travelled and worked and joked, month in and month out, around the world. They brought me, in particular, one friend who was to become a boon companion.

I had just arrived in Bombay and, following the civilized custom of tropical countries, had retired to bed after luncheon for a siesta. As I lay perspiring and half asleep, beneath my mosquito net, with nothing but a loincloth to cover me, I became vaguely aware of a tall figure looming beside my bed, through the dim half-light of the hot afternoon. I turned around and recognized a young Indian Cavalry officer who had been selected from the Indian Army to serve as my A.D.C., and, as I remembered, had been presented to me on the quayside that morning. His name was Captain Edward Dudley Metcalfe.

Without ceremony or apology for intruding on my

slumbers, he sat down, there and then, on a chair beside me, and began earnestly to talk, with a slight Irish brogue. Very soon I was sitting up. For he was talking about polo. How would I like to play polo in India? I would like it very much. All right, I had but to say the word and he would fix it. He knew a number of maharajahs who were eager to lend me ponies. Thus, in a day or so, I had a trainload of thirty polo ponies complete with native grooms, or *sayces*, at the exclusive disposal of myself and my staff. Wherever we went, they now followed us, accommodated in horse-boxes in a special train of their own. And whenever time and place allowed—which was mercifully often—we played polo.

My father soon tumbled to this new pursuit of mine, and began to write to me: 'I see you are playing polo a good deal, I hope you don't overdo the exercise in that climate' . . . 'I was sorry to hear you got a crack over the eye from the ball while playing polo. . . . Considering the number of times you have played polo, I think it very lucky that you haven't been hit before.'

It was thus polo that started my friendship with 'Fruity' Metcalfe, which was to endure until his death, thirty-six years later. Of all my friends, it was he alone, with his informal and expansive Irish nature, who behaved towards me, not as though I were a Prince, but as though I were an ordinary human being like himself. He always referred to me as 'The Little Man'. People were sometimes shocked by the familiarity of his attitude towards me, as when once, riding beside me in the hunting field, needing to light a cigarette and having damped his match-box, he light-heartedly struck a match on the sole of my boot—an impulsive and characteristic gesture which amused and delighted me.

Fruity gave up his job in India to join my staff as an Equerry, accompanying me on the rest of my Eastern tour and so back to London. Here he had a room at York House, St. James's Palace. My life was a busy one, involving me in an endless round of public engagements, not only in London but in all parts of the country. But on evenings off from official dinners, or after them, Fruity and I would go out and have a good time.

Our evenings usually began with a cocktail in York House. These cocktails were far too strong at first, since Finch, now my butler, who had looked after me since childhood and was conservative in his habits, refused flatly to put ice into drinks. He declared that the ice would bruise the gin. It was only after his retirement that my cocktails became reasonably iced and diluted.

Later in the evening, after dinner and maybe a show, we would go around the West End of London with a small group of friends, often dancing until the small hours of the morning to the lively jazz bands of the Roaring 'Twenties. The private balls of that period, in the great houses that still survived, tended, with a few notable exceptions, to be rather formal affairs, at which I had to watch my step before the older generation of my father's friends. They seem to have kept him pretty well informed, not only on my deportment but on my costume as well. One morning he greeted me with the words: 'I hear you were not wearing gloves at the ball last night. Please see that this does not occur again.'

But this was the 'Golden Age' of the restaurant and the night club, often with floor show, and I would escape to the Embassy Club, that Buckingham Palace of night clubs, the Kit-Cat, Quaglino's or the Café de Paris, with its 'Champagne and Chandeliers', which I am told that I helped, by my patronage, to save at a moment when it was faced with a deficit of some thousands of pounds.

Afterwards we would sometimes continue the party at York House. I remember an evening when Fred and Adèle Astaire, at that time drawing large audiences in London, danced for us there to the gramophone. I remember another evening when Paul Whiteman's Band made its first appearance at the Grafton Galleries. The men of our party included all three of my brothers and inevitably Fruity, who danced most of the evening with 'Baba' Curzon, later to become his wife.

When the restaurant closed, we still wanted to go on dancing. The problem was, where? We could hardly take the whole of Paul Whiteman's Band back to York House. Lady Alexandra, however, made a bold suggestion—that we should go to the house of her father, Lord Curzon, in Carlton House Terrace. Lord Curzon, then Foreign Secretary, was abroad at the time on the nation's business, and the house was empty and servantless, but for a caretaker.

Baba went ahead, fetched some champagne from York House and ripped the dust sheets off the furniture in Carlton House Terrace. The Band followed and we danced through the night until 6 a.m., drinking champagne mostly from the tooth-glasses in the bathrooms, which were all that the daughter of the house had been able to find for us. Our enjoyment was perhaps enhanced by the sense of truancy that we felt at so using the house of the august Lord Curzon who was always, in his ways, *plus royaliste que le Roi*.

All would have been well and he might never have known of our nocturnal invasion but for an unfortunate accident. My brother Harry (now the Duke of Gloucester), a man of some weight, sat casually on His Lordship's dining-room table—and broke it in two. The reason for this disaster had, of course, to be explained to Lord Curzon—and the story was out. It was Lady Curzon, Baba's stepmother, who undertook this task and she did so with such tact and diplomacy that no unfortunate repercussions followed.

On the morning after that party, Baba and my brother George changed straight away into their tweeds, without going to bed, and went off to play a round of golf; while Fruity did the same, and went off to try out a horse which I was thinking of buying. I used to call him my 'Master of the Horse' since he now looked after all my hunters and steeplechasers, as he had looked after my horses and ponies in India, and as an expert in horseflesh he advised me on every purchase.

One morning, after dancing all night at another party in Lord Curzon's house—this time a fancy-dress ball at which Fruity and I were dressed as Japanese Coolies—we went down to Aldershot together for a ride with the Draghounds. I had sent down a new hunter, which I was all for riding. But Fruity always preferred to try out a horse himself before I rode it. So, ignoring my protests, he mounted and rode off after the hounds. The horse took the first fence by the roots, crashed right through it and threw Fruity on to a half-made road of jagged flints. The same accident would undoubtedly have happened to me had I been on its back.

I picked him up unconscious, and he was removed to London in an ambulance with his nose broken and his face terribly lacerated. He spent some time in hospital, where the noted plastic surgeon, Sir Harold Gillies, performed a skilful operation on his face with the aid of photographs as a guide, and restored his nose to its previous splendour; and Fruity emerged from hospital quite as handsome and irresistible to the opposite sex as he ever was before.

It was a sad day for Fruity as well as myself, when I had, in deference to my father, to give up much of my riding, including all point-to-point racing, and he left my service to return to India, as A.D.C. to the Commander-in-Chief, Sir William Birdwood. What I felt about riding in these days is reflected in a letter I once wrote to him from Balmoral, after a day spent in pursuit of my father's stags:

> But stalking seems very tame after riding as everything else does and I'm missing my riding terribly and hope to God I won't lose the very little I feel I've picked up in the last 6 weeks!! And what about all my lovely boots? I feel that every step I take on the hill is making my chances of getting into them again smaller and smaller!!! This feeling haunts me!!

The boots today lie, well-enough tended among my possessions at Frogmore.

Fruity Metcalfe, was, in a sense, my 'Master of the Wardrobe' as well. In his discreet way he was a dandy or maybe I should say a 'buck'. To be turned out well was to him a matter of great importance. It was a standing joke at White's Club that, if you followed Fruity down Bond Street, he might stop at intervals and look into the shop windows to adjust his tie, hat, and handkerchief. At Craven Lodge we would spend many minutes—though perhaps not so many as Beau Brummell—in front of the mirror struggling to tie our hunting stocks to perfection. He was, in a sense, my Beau Brummell, in that he advised me critically on my clothes.

Fruity tended to be conservative over matters of colour. He used to try to restrain my tastes, when Mr. Stanford, of Hawes and Curtis, laid before us the latest and brightest shirts and sweaters. He would often appeal against my choice to Mr. Stanford, who would reply diplomatically: 'Perhaps there's something in what the Major says.' This became a key-phrase in my exchanges with Fruity. Often, when he offered me advice or criticism on a matter of any kind, as he seldom hesitated to, he would add, with a wag of the finger: 'There's something in what the Major says!'

However, I sometimes disagreed with his advice, as I fancy the Prince Regent seldom did with Brummell's; nor can I claim to have in any way emulated my royal forbear's dandyish standards. George IV's wardrobe, at his death, was valued at £15,000. As Mr. James Laver recalls, he would spend £800 on a cloak alone, while he left to his heirs some hundreds of waistcoats, many of which had never been worn.

My own wardrobe as a Prince, during the nineteen-twenties, was by comparison modest. My expenditure amounted, nevertheless, to a good deal more than that of the well-dressed Regency gentleman, who could in terms of the currency of the time dress for less than £50 a year, while it was possible to be quite decently dressed for half that sum.

When I was a young man at Oxford, living, since my father's Accession to the Throne, on the revenues of the Duchy of Cornwall, its Secretary, Mr. Walter Peacock, in presenting me with a summary of my personal expenditure for the years 1911 to 1913, paid me the compliment of writing that my bills 'all seem very reasonable and I don't think that anyone could say that Your Royal

Highness is extravagant. While there is no waste, I feel sure that any impartial person would say that everything is done on generous lines, which is as it should be'. He added that, after the payment of £2,000 for my initial overall Oxford expenses, tailors' and hosiers' bills had been steadily decreasing, but were bound to increase in future—as indeed they did.

Mr. Peacock, later Sir Walter, could not, of course, foresee the First World War, when I spent relatively little. After the war, however, my manifold activities in public and in private, at home and abroad, now called, if I was to maintain sartorial standards approaching those which Queen Victoria and the Prince Consort had laid down for their eldest son, for a substantial outlay on clothes.

From 1919 until 1959—a space of forty years—my principal tailor in London was Scholte. It is a firm which, alas, no longer exists. Mr. Scholte died soon after the Second World War, during which his premises were badly bombed, and his son, who inherited the business, gave it up on the expiry of the lease last year. It was one of my Equerries who first introduced me to this august establishment in Savile Row, as gentlemanly and discreet in its atmosphere as any London Club.

Scholte, who came originally from Holland, was a tailor of the old school, who had run his own business since my grandfather's time. He once told me that as a young man he had had to serve ten years of arduous apprenticeship before he was allowed to cut a suit for a client. He had the strictest ideas as to how a gentleman should and should not be dressed. In the Brummell tradition, he disapproved strongly of any form of exaggeration in the style of a coat. He steadfastly refused to make clothes for the theatre and later for the film world, making exceptions only in the cases of Sir Charles Hawtrey and Sir Allan Aynesworth, whom he regarded as sufficiently restrained in their tastes to qualify for Scholte suits—and then only off-stage.

I was present in his shop when he refused to cut a suit for Fruity Metcalfe—much to that gallant officer's mortification, and to my own secret amusement. As befitted an artist and craftsman, Scholte had rigid standards concerning the perfect balance of proportions between shoulders and waist in the cut of a coat to clothe the masculine torso. Fruity who, for all his discretion of costume was always ready for some experiment, had sinned by demanding wider shoulders and a narrower waist. Thus for a time he was excluded from Scholte's sacred precints.

These peculiar proportions were Scholte's secret formula. His rivals would aspire in vain to have suits made for them without disclosing their identity, so that they could take them to pieces and, by measuring, discover the secret. But they never succeeded. Scholte knew his clients, and remained alertly on his guard. He used to recall one Saturday when a flashy gentleman in a sports car drew up before his shop and began to order some suits. But Scholte recognized his type at once, and politely refused to make for him. He was, as he afterwards discovered, a wholesale tailor from the Seven Sisters Road.

It was for another reason that he refused, on one occasion, to make for an American Ambassador to Britain. The Ambassador needed a morning-coat in a hurry for a royal garden party. But when he came to try it on, he made the mistake of bringing his wife along with him. The Ambassadress began to find fault with the cut and the hang of the coat, and to suggest improvements. Scholte, without comment, removed the coat from the Ambassador's back, flung it on the floor, and refused to complete it. The Ambassador returned next day, without his wife, and, in view of his urgent need for the coat, implored him to reconsider this drastic decision. Scholte relented, and agreed to complete the job, adding, however, in a burst of undiplomatic Dutch bluntness: 'But don't bring that damned woman in here again!'

That Scholte could make clothes in a hurry, if need be, I discovered for myself one summer, when I appeared at Ascot wearing a dark grey morning-coat with trousers to match. I never cared much for the black morning-coat, disliking always those 'fancy pants', of a striped pattern, that inevitably went with it. Sometimes I compromised by wearing trousers of a close shepherd's plaid check pattern instead.

But I preferred the morning-suit, with coat and trousers all of a single shade of grey. I remember admiring the elegance of Lord Reading, who as Viceroy of India always dressed in a light grey frock-coat suit of this kind. Mr. Lloyd George, I recall, used to wear, a shade less elegantly, similar suits with matching morning-coat and trousers. But he would often wear a bowler hat with them or even a Homburg—a solecism undreamt of in the top-hatted post-war age.

Anyway, here I was at Ascot, looking my smartest, I liked to think, in my grey morning-coat. Unfortunately I had forgotten something: The Court was in mourning for some distant relative. On reaching the racecourse, I thus earned rebuke from my father, who pointed out that in the circumstances a black morning-coat was required.

But to my dismay, I realized that, for some reason or another, I did not possess one.

I called Scholte from the racecourse throwing myself at his mercy, and telling him that I should require a new black morning-coat for the next day's racing, but that I should be unable to get to London until nearly six o'clock that evening. On arriving I drove straight to his shop, chose the material, had my measurements checked and returned to Windsor where I was stopping.

Scholte himself cut out the coat there and then, and handed it to one of his tailors, who had stayed behind after the shop was closed. He sat up half the night making the coat. In the morning it arrived at Windsor complete. It was a perfect fit, and I drove over to Ascot secure in the knowledge that I was now correctly and respectfully dressed.

With this formal costume I always preferred the grey top hat. I have been told that I helped to make it popular, by wearing it at Ascot, where a black silk hat is seldom seen today. The silk hat was nevertheless a smart enough form of headgear when it first appeared in the early nineteenth century, derived, as Mr. Laver has pointed out, from the stove-pipe 'crash-helmet' of the hunting man. George III, in the half-length black silk hat, with cockade like a coachman's, which he wore with his Windsor uniform for his portrait by Stroehling, cuts a truly royal figure; and so did my father and grandfather in theirs. But the time had come, I felt, to adapt this traditional form of headgear to a lighter, brighter age. Moreover, the grey top hat had a more practical advantage. It did not require reblocking.

It was one of Scholte's rules that his clients, whoever they might be, must come to his shop for their fittings.

He refused to visit them at home. I always obeyed this rule, and never, except for some exceptional reason, asked for a fitting at York House. I was thus departing from the accepted custom of royalty. I cannot imagine King George V in a London shop. His tradesmen always came to him. My mother, on the other hand, loved to shop, especially for antiques, and her Daimler was a familiar sight in London, drawn up by the kerb of some busy shopping street, with a small crowd gathered on the pavement to watch her emerge, with her upright carriage and her gracious smile. I must have inherited this taste from her, since I have always enjoyed popping in and out of stores and selecting what I want on the spot.

Otherwise, I imagine that few of the Royal Warrant Holders, whose dinner I once had the pleasure of attending, can boast that a King has ever set foot in their premises. As Prince of Wales, I was entitled to issue these royal warrants, which can be granted to a firm after three years' service, but which as King I was never able to do, since I reigned for less than three years. The list of my 'Prince of Wales's Warrants' contains the names of some thirty tradesmen, ranging beyond London to an optician in Calcutta, a cartage contractor in Portsmouth, a cigarette-maker in Malta, a photographer in Southsea, a chemist in Sunningdale, and several tradesmen in Oxford.

The Prince Consort once conferred an exceptional honour on his private tailor, a man named Edward Peacock, who had first attracted his attention while singing before him as a choirboy at a soirée in St. Martin's Lane. He allowed him to display the Royal Coat of Arms without the official warrant. When my grandfather came to the throne, the Warrant Holders took exception to this, and removed his name from the list. But Mr. Peacock wrote personally to the King, and received the reply that he might continue for the rest of his life—which His Majesty hoped would be a long one—to use the Coat of Arms.

Michael Arlen wrote an entertaining novel called *Mayfair*, in which he created a tailoring firm called Messrs. Sleep and Sluis. They could 'build a white waistcoat about a waist in a way that was a wonder to the eye. By Royal Appointment and rightly'. He refers later in the book to Conduit Street as 'a shocking street for trousers'.

I never had a pair of trousers made by Scholte. I disliked his cut of them; they were made, as English trousers usually are, to be worn with braces high above the waist. So preferring as I did to wear a belt rather than braces with trousers, in the American style, I invariably had them made by another tailor.

During the war, when I was Governor of the Bahamas, my wardrobe began to wear out, and on a visit to New York I decided to replenish it. I went to a tailor named Harris, who had served his apprenticeship in London. I gave him a pair of my old London trousers and he copied them admirably. Since then, I have had my trousers made in New York and my coats in London, an international compromise which the Duchess aptly describes as 'pants across the sea'.

I am, I gather, in good company, since Brummell himself had his coat made by one tailor, his waistcoat by another, and his breeches by a third. He had one advantage over me, however. He did not have to go all the way across the Atlantic for the breeches.

CHAPTER X

CHANGES IN FASHION

Wars, as Mr. James Laver has remarked, are fought nowadays in sports clothes. A friend of mine recalls a period during the last war when Field-Marshal Lord Alexander held a daily conference for his staff officers on the Italian front. Things were quiet at that time; there was little to confer on. But the staff, of which my friend was a member, went to these conferences all the same—not so much to hear what the Field-Marshal would say, as to see what he would wear. He had a dashing line in corduroys, battle-dress blouses, suède boots, berets and such.

In the First World War, officers adhered more strictly to the regulation uniform. We allowed ourselves nevertheless a few variations in the field service dress. There was, for example, the 'British Warm', that comfortable half-length great-coat, whose life was prolonged, in the interests of economy, into the post-war period. Then there was the 'Fielding Coat', devised by Major-General Sir Geoffrey Fielding, who commanded the Guards Division. This was a roomier version of the

In 1914 I was an ensign in the Grenadier Guards

Punting on the river at Oxford, when I was at Magdalen College

Relaxing during a golf game at Le Touquet in 1924

Talking with footballers

Inspecting an O.T.C. unit

With President Alvear, driving through Buenos Aires in 1925

Discussing with Admiral Fitzmaurice my wrist, which had become swollen owing to too much handshaking during my visit to Cape Town

At Ladysmith in 1925, presenting a cane to the Chief of Basutoland

Hunting in Leicestershire in the conventional pink coat and hard topper

officers' field-service dress-jacket, plentifully equipped with extra pockets and made of a corded material.

It was not of course until after the war that it became possible for a man to display anything like an individual taste in dress. And this, if I am to believe my Equerries, I began to do. Each day, they tell me, they would await my morning appearances with eager anticipation, and in their minds the question 'What will he be wearing this time?'

This became equally a matter of some interest to the daily Press, who were always quick to notice any eccentricity in my costume, foreshadowing, for example, the birth of a new fashion from the fact that, having changed in a hurry, I wore turned-up trousers with a morning-coat, or that, one cold evening, I slipped on a sweater beneath my double-breasted dinner-jacket. I may indeed have helped, in my modest way, to launch some new fashions. But they certainly were not these.

All my life, hitherto, I had been fretting against those constrictions of dress which reflected my family's world of rigid social convention. It was my impulse, whenever I found myself alone, to remove my coat, rip off my tie, loosen my collar and roll up my sleeves—a gesture aspiring not merely to comfort but, in a more symbolic sense, to freedom. The Duchess likes to describe this process as my 'striptease act'. It can have embarrassing implications when guests are expected. I like to remain thus coatless and tieless until the last possible moment. So to avoid being caught out by them, I often have to sneak out of one door as they are coming in at another, while a servant brings the clothes to me outside, enabling me to appear a minute later before my guests, dressed as a host should be. When working at my desk, without a coat, I often, when it is cold, put on instead an old light golfing-jacket of blue, with white over check, cut like a battle-dress blouse. The Duchess calls this my 'thinking coat'.

Comfort and freedom were the two principles that underlay the change in male fashions throughout the freer and easier democratic age between the First World War and the Second. It was a change, however, which after the manner of the conservative male, happened gradually, discreetly, indeed in a sense imperceptibly. Typical of it was, in the first place, the lounge-suit—its very name suggesting ease—which now became the universal dress for men. Its jacket had grown gradually out of the morning-coat, whose tails, by the end of the nineteenth century, were sometimes shortened to a point below the hip, until they disappeared altogether, giving place to a long skirted coat, with a slit up the back. Earlier in the century it had appeared as a sports jacket, but not yet as an urban garment. At first the lounge jacket buttoned high at the neck, but gradually the number of buttons diminished from four to three, to two, and even—though not in the best circles—to one.

Concurrently, the double-breasted lounge jacket, which had originated in the naval reefer, became more popular, the number of its effective buttons likewise diminishing from six to four. The waistcoat, which had already been getting lower at the neck, now began to seem superfluous and, in the end, disappeared altogether. Eventually the braces went too, being replaced by the belt, and the masculine frame was once and for all freed.

Meanwhile, trousers had grown wider, hence looser, than they had been in the Edwardian drainpipe age—even on the legs of my father, conservative as he was in his clothes. The young men at Oxford, to the stern disapproval of Scholte, widened them to as much as twenty inches, so that they resembled a pair of elephant's legs. 'From such like excesses,' prayed the *Tailor and Cutter*, 'good Lord deliver us.' Once, when I went into Scholte's to try on a coat, he looked severely at my legs and remarked: 'I hope you are not going in for those Oxford bags.' I reassured him, pointing out that my trousers were only an inch or so wider than I had worn them before.

The fashion of 'Oxford bags' gradually died. They were, however, worn for some time on the golf course, in the interests of leg-room, by the noted amateur player, Rex Hartley, who had been captain, oddly enough, not of Oxford but of Cambridge, and they may have played their part, thanks to him and others, in the eventual demise of plus-fours, and the adoption of trousers as the standard dress for golf. There is however one noted golfer who still remains faithful to plus-fours: Gene Sarazen, British and American Open Champion in the early nineteen-thirties. Once when I asked him why, he replied, 'Because I have so many pairs that I have to wear them out!'

But while the suits of the male grew freer and more comfortable, the real revolution in his costume came with the gradual ending of the tyranny of starch. The soft shirt had already arrived. Soft collars and cuffs now came to be worn as a matter of course, and the shirt without collar attached began to die a slow, natural death. When this softening-up process began to extend even to evening-dress, that was a revolution indeed.

It had already begun by 1928, when I found myself

making a rather fanciful speech at the annual banquet of the Jewellers and Silversmiths' Association at Birmingham. 'Have any of you,' I asked, 'ever stopped to think why we are all dressed up in these stiff armour-plated shirts tonight? I believe they originated in this way. A hundred years back, men wore soft pleated shirts of an evening, and then the steam laundries and steam mangles were invented, and men found that their beautiful shirts were returned to them with buttons ground to the most useless fragments. So evening shirt-front studs were invented. But shirt studs won't stay put in a soft shirt. And so our ancestors very rashly decided to have the fronts of their shirts starched. So, gentlemen, we have first of all the laundries and then we have the jewellers to blame for the 'boiled shirt'—for it is this horrible garment we have to wear now which has given us such untold misery.'

The relief of this misery took time. Throughout the greater part of the 'twenties the evening tail-coat, requiring the boiled shirt, reigned supreme. For several years after the war it was still worn even at private dinners, while at the smarter restaurants and night-clubs which I used to frequent, it was the absolute rule. But the dinner-jacket was slowly but inexorably making inroads on masculine conservatism, a progress gently assisted by my brother George and myself. It was a garment which my grandfather had first worn in his later days as Prince of Wales, but only for very small private dinners. The habit is said to have arisen from the informal mess dress, consisting of a dark blue cloth jacket with silk facings and gilt buttons, which he wore aboard the *Serapis* on his voyage to India.

Now however the dinner-jacket came out into the open and, by the end of the 'twenties, it was being worn as a matter of course by myself and my friends for supper in the Embassy Club and other such places of amusement. We took to having it made—and the dress-coat too—in a midnight blue cloth, in place of black, thus unconsciously following my grandfather's practice. At first, as a concession to formality, I used to wear it with a white waistcoat, a new fashion which became popular for a time, and which in a sense echoed, in up-to-date terms, my grandfather's establishment of the white waistcoat in place of the black as the correct dress with a tail-coat.

But, in the meantime, a new version of this evening garment had appeared—the double-breasted dinner-jacket. It had first been worn in London, I believe, by dance-band leaders, coming from the United States, while Jack Buchanan had sung and danced in it on the stage. But it was regarded a little askance in more conventional circles until granted royal grace and favour by that most elegant of monarchs, King Alfonso of Spain. My brother and I started to wear it when we went out in the evenings, often with a plain dark-red carnation in the lapel, the flower which had taken the place of the more elaborate mixed buttonholes of my father's and grandfather's time. When we first did so, we were marking, without being at first aware of it, a new stage in the softening-up of the severities of masculine attire.

Already I had taken to wearing a soft shirt, with a single-breasted dinner-jacket, and if my shirt was stiff, my cuffs were now often soft. I was still faithful to the stiff collar, but it was usually of the comfortable turned-down variety. Even the stuck-up variety, which I wore with a dress-coat, had relaxed its grip on the throat muscles and spread its wings, while the bow-tie had sprung up from beneath to cover them, a practice which arose, like so many of the most desirable fashions, by mistake. The perpetrator of this happy error, was I believe, a head waiter who, changing in a hurry one evening, found that he had tied his white tie over the points of his collar instead of under them. The practice was immediately followed by Nelson Keys, who, like Jack Buchanan, was, on a miniature scale, one of the 'bucks' of the stage.

As a result, the bows of our ties grew bigger and broader, whether shaped like thistle or bats-wing. They grew moreover simpler to knot. The single-ended tie was born, thus killing for ever the stock joke of the gentleman struggling before the mirror to tie his tie while already late for dinner. Another innovation, in the interests of more rapid dress, was to have all my shirts made with collars attached.

Meanwhile, however, we began to find that, with the double-breasted dinner-jacket, a soft collar looked just as neat as a stiff one, and by the 'thirties, we were all beginning to 'dress soft', thus combining as no previous generation had done sartorial dignity with comfort and ease. Thus the evening reign, following the day reign, of starch was at last shaken to its foundations. Today it is a monarch which rules only over the most formal—rightly named the starchiest—of social occasions.

Another reign was equally shaken: that of the evening waistcoat. Already it had dwindled to minute proportions, a garment which my grandfather, with his ample white expanses of waistcoat, would hardly have recognized as such. At first it had abandoned the sweeping curve of its neckline for a more matter-of-fact V-shape, buttoning low and leaving itself with a mere three buttons and hardly more inches of material to cover the waist. More drastically still, the backless waistcoat was born, freeing the male back from its previous excess of material.

It was an innovation which I took up with alacrity, discussing it, as I always discussed such matters of moment, with my haberdasher, Hawes and Curtis. Fred Astaire, in his memoirs, recalls an evening spent with me and a party of friends at a night club. He happened to notice the lapels of my white waistcoat, which were of a special design, and the fact that it did not show beneath the front of my dress-coat. Next morning he went into Hawes and Curtis, and asked for a waistcoat made in the same style. He was told, apologetically, that this could not be supplied. So he went into another shop, which agreed to make one for him.

If ever I wear a waistcoat today, whether with day or with evening clothes, it is backless still. But, except with a dress-suit, I seldom do so. The double-breasted dinner-jacket, like the double-breasted lounge-jacket, made the waistcoat unnecessary and I very soon dropped it. Today, in the evenings, the more comfortable cummerbund, sometimes worn by the Victorians on a hot summer day, is taking its place.

London in those days of my youth was a city, if not perhaps of dandies as in previous ages, then at least of men who dressed with distinction. Some affected a flamboyance of dress which in spirit belonged rather to a past generation. One of these was Lord Lonsdale, a contemporary of my father, who was known as 'the Yaller' or 'the Yellow Earl' from the fact that everything around him—his cars, his carriages, the liveries of his servants—was canary yellow in colour. Even his horses were as yellow as a horse can get: they were invariably of a light shade of chestnut. As these vivid tastes suggest, Lord Lonsdale had few inhibitions about showing off. I remember a Derby at Epsom when rain had fallen and there was some doubt about the state of the course.

'How's the going, Hugh?' my father asked him.

'I shall find out, Your Majesty,' he replied.

He found out by walking on to the course, calling upon a Mounted Police officer to dismount, getting on to his horse, and cantering past the stands, to the delight of the crowd, in all the glory of his race-going regalia.

Lord Lonsdale, as befitted one of his generation, favoured the frock-coat—but a frock-coat of so individual a cut that the *Tailor and Cutter* once described it as positively 'a sartorial sensation'. He liked to wear bright colours. His shirt was often of pink, or of white with pink stripes, like bars of candy running across them in a horizontal direction. With this he liked to wear a white waistcoat and even, on a hot day, a pair of white duck trousers. Sometimes he preferred a tie in his own racing colours. For less formal functions he would wear a short tail-coat, of the type worn in past generations for shooting, with large pocket flaps at the waist.

Another of these flamboyant sportsmen was Sir Walter Gilbey, who attracted attention on the racecourse chiefly by the dashing style of his top hats and bowlers. He had them specially made for him, with brims which curled with a provocative flourish. He also made a cult of fancy waistcoats, which he accumulated with the zest of a collector, wearing them always with buttons engraved with his initials.

Another picturesque figure was Lord Londonderry, who looked every inch a lord, but a lord of the past, with silk facings and cuffs on his morning-coat, a high starched collar and a voluminous black silk stock, not far removed in its style from the cravats worn by his ancestor, Lord Castlereagh, in the portrait by Lawrence at Windsor.

My brother-in-law, the late Lord Harewood, was always well, if conservatively dressed. He affected especially high stiff collars, rounded instead of pointed and with so narrow an opening as to leave little room for the knot of the tie. He must have had a large wardrobe. On one occasion, after the war, he sent a new suit back to Scholte with the complaint that, in unpacking it for the first time, his valet had found it to be very badly creased. Scholte sent it back to him, impeccably pressed, accounting for the previous creases by the fact that the suit had been made for him and delivered in 1911, ten years before.

More casual and tweeded in appearance was Colonel Fred Cripps, who had his clothes cut loose, in a countrified style. He liked to wear an Inverness cape even in London. His father, incongruously enough, was a Socialist peer, Lord Parmoor, while his brother was Sir Stafford, the Socialist Chancellor. I remember an evening during a general election, when Fred, looking characteristically opulent, surprised an elegant group of friends at the Embassy Club by remarking, in his rather mincing accent: '*Ai* vote Socialist.'

If dress is an art, it is also a trade. All these smart young men of the period were used by the clothing industry as unconscious models for the propagation of

British fashions and the sale of British products all over the world, and especially in America. A tailor or shirt-maker would try out a new material or a new style on one of them and see how it went before putting it into production. I myself played a fairly prominent and for the most part equally unconscious role in this process. After all it was part of my job as Prince of Wales to support and to stimulate British trade in general, and this inevitably included men's clothes.

It is impossible to name, seriously, the best-dressed or even the ten best-dressed men in the world. There are different styles, and certain men who wear each of them well. The details of a man's costume are a matter of individual taste—whether his lapels be broad or narrow or his trousers long or short. I prefer four buttons on my coat sleeves, for example, but I cannot give any logical reason why I do. Even one button would seem to be superfluous. Yet I am credited with having influenced styles in my time. It was quite unconscious; I have always tried to dress to my own individual taste.

I was in fact 'produced' as a leader of fashion, with the clothiers as my showmen and the world as my audience. The middle-man in this process was the photographer, employed not only by the Press but by the trade, whose task it was to photograph me on every possible occasion, public or private, with an especial eye for what I happened to be wearing. A selection of these photographs, together with patterns of materials and samples of collars, ties, socks, waistcoats, and so forth, was immediately rushed to America, where overnight a new fashion might well be born—to the considerable advantage of the British export trade.

An extreme instance of this spirit of imitation, which is after all the sincerest form of flattery, was provided by an American from Chicago, who left a standing order with Scholte in London, for a replica of every suit I ordered. Another lavish imitator was a South American, who, after my tour as a species of trade ambassador to his country, the Argentine, came to London, ordered thirty-five suits from a tailor, and paid for all of them in cash. Twenty of them were plus-four suits which, as a result of my visit, became the accepted country wear of the Argentinians.

A more widespread success was enjoyed by the Brigade of Guards tie. As a former officer of the Grenadier Guards, with whom I had served during the war, I had the right to wear this tie and often did so. The fashion spotters were quick to notice this, and within a year of the Armistice the tie, with its broad blue and red stripes, had become the rage in America. It is still popular among Americans, who like to wear British regimental and old school ties, blissfully regardless of any right to do so.

Blissfully ignorant of their origin too! Once in Washington, a reporter caught up with me and asked me what tie I was wearing. I replied: 'The Guards tie.' Not seeming to understand me correctly, he repeated the question. 'What kind of a tie?' I answered him again: 'The Guards tie.' Misunderstanding my pronunciation he settled for 'Gawd's tie'. Afterwards he wrote in his column that I had 'left this reporter doubtful as to whether the Almighty had actually ever devised a tie of his own'.

The most surprising place where I encountered the

Guards tie was in Sweden. When invited to play golf at the club of Falsterbo, near Malmö, in 1932, I noticed that all the members were wearing it. I was wearing it too, as they themselves noticed. Over drinks after the game I jokingly accused them of appopriating a tie to which they had no right. They retorted by making the same accusation against me. This, they explained, was the tie of their club, of which I was not a member. I immediately took off my tie and presented it to the Captain, who then took off his and presented it to me. And so honour was satisfied.

The so-called 'Windsor knot' in the tie was adopted in America at a later date. It was I believe regulation wear for G.I.s during the war, when American college boys adopted it too. But in fact I was in no way responsible for this. The knot to which the Americans gave my name was a double knot in a narrow tie—a 'Slim Jim' as it is sometimes called. It is true that I myself have always preferred a large knot, as looking better than a small one, so during the nineteen-twenties I devised, in conclave with Mr. Sandford, a tie always of the broad variety which was reinforced by an extra thickness of material to produce this effect. As far as I know this particular fashion has never been followed in America or elsewhere.

Americans have also shown an interest in other British accessories. An American friend of mine in Palm Beach, Christopher Dunphy, founded a 'button club' and did me the honour of making me a member. The members are required to wear on their sports coats such gilt or silver buttons as they have been able to find. A few years ago, a local antique dealer bought up a stock of old buttons such as retainers wore, from the liveries of British families, and he did a good trade selling them to members of Christopher's club.

This gave me an idea. Back in France, I selected some of my old regimental and hunt buttons, which I had sewn on my sports jackets. When I returned to Palm Beach the following year I showed them to the antique dealer, remarking: 'Here are some *real* buttons. Buttons I am entitled to wear.' His face showed consternation. A few days later he anxiously pleaded with the Duchess: 'I do hope the Duke will keep quiet about his buttons or he will ruin my trade.'

Considering its emphasis on progress in every direction, I have always found that America is in many ways a country deeply rooted in tradition. Pride of State and of City, with a respect for the past, run high. Take for example the Duchess's home town of Baltimore in the State of Maryland. Each year, its leading citizens hold an Assembly Ball of a highly formal and exclusive nature. At this ball, for which full evening dress with white kid gloves is worn by ladies and gentlemen alike, only a member of the Assembly committee is permitted to dance or to invite a lady to do so. Thus, though I have had the privilege of attending the Assembly, I have never been able to enjoy a dance there.

An annual hunt ball is also held in Baltimore, on the night of the Maryland Hunt Cup meeting. For this, following the custom, I put on a pink hunt coat. On its lapels I wear the light blue watered-silk facings of the Quorn. At the last ball we attended, the Duchess, who has a keen feminine eye for such details, noticed that the silk was distinctly frayed. So I brought the coat back to

London to be refaced, creating something of a problem for Scholte. He had some difficulty in finding the traditional watered-silk, and was afraid that he might have to substitute plain silk. But he found a piece of it in the end as, knowing his persistence, I felt sure he would do.

New Yorkers—at least those among whom I spend most of my time—tend to be as conservative in their clothes as Londoners. There are, it is true, certain subtle distinctions between the two. A friend of mine from the Eastern seaboard, a tall upstanding gentleman whom I have always regarded as more British than the British both in his apparel and in his accent, was in a London club one day, waiting for a member who had invited him for lunch. As he stood at the bar he overheard three young men speculating as to whether he was an American or an Englishman. He could not resist approaching them with the question, 'Which do you really think I am?'

Two of them replied that they thought he was British. But the third dubbed him an American. Asked how he had come to this conclusion, he said, 'Because of your tie.'

'You have ruined my life!' my friend exclaimed. He had thought this tie of his to be of the discreetest and most British design. Now, whenever he goes to London, he finds himself looking curiously at every man's tie before he looks at his face, trying in bewilderment to discover just how he went wrong.

However formally they may be dressed, Americans do tend to wear brighter ties than the British do. They also wear, rather more often, their own versions of the old school and club ties. There are many, of course, who wear those gaily painted ties, on which it is possible to have anything portrayed, from a skull and crossbones to the image and name of a sweetheart. But these are not, on the whole, numbered among my friends.

There are differences between the two races in other such details of dress. I myself like, for example, when I dress in the morning, to see that my tie, socks, shirt and handkerchief tone, more or less, with the suit I have chosen. I have not noticed many Americans who match up their clothes in this way. Often I have seen them wearing, say, a blue suit with a fawn shirt, red tie and green socks. I have one American friend, the president of a big corporation, who goes to the opposite extreme. He likes to wear shirt, tie and handkerchief of precisely the same checked pattern. This, maybe, is carrying conformity a little too far. These various accessories of masculine costume should, in my view, blend, but they should not match too exactly. This, I suppose, is an instance of the notorious British convention of understatement, expressed in terms of clothes.

The costume of the New York businessman is not perhaps so strict a 'uniform' as that of his London counterpart. But I have noticed one curious thing about him. He seldom, if ever, wears that short black jacket with 'fancy pants' which our more conservative professional men still favour, but whatever suit he may be wearing, he is apt to put on for wear in his office a pair of black socks, such as I myself wear with evening dress alone.

Such variations of dress as exist between Britain and America derive mainly from differences of climate. America is climatically a land of extremes, of very cold winters and very hot summers. In New York, when I venture out in the streets in the winter, I almost always put on a heavy, fur-lined overcoat. The one I prefer is made of a grey-patterned tweed, and is lined with a nutria pelt from one of the Duchess's discarded fur coats. It is so heavy that the 'hat check' girls wince and wilt when they lift it off my shoulders.

It is lighter, nevertheless, than another of my overcoats. Fur-lined too, but with an Astrakhan collar, I wear this one less often, because of its cut which suggests rather the fashions of an earlier age. For it hangs in pleats from the waist downwards, and reaches almost to my ankles, as low as those overcoats which London cabbies used to wear in my youth. My grandfather, who liked to wear a coat with an Astrakhan collar, might not have scorned this one of mine. In fact it was given to me, in the nineteen-thirties, by my old friend and Equerry, General Trotter—a replica of a coat which he wore himself, and for which I had always expressed admiration.

But it is the hot summers rather than the cold winters of the United States that dictate American clothes; and above all it is the central heating and air-conditioning which create indoors a constant climate, summer and winter alike.

In my youth of course—in Britain at least—such amenities were virtually unknown. When, on my father's death, my mother moved from Buckingham Palace into Marlborough House, it had no heating system of any kind. The Office of Works, in preparing the house for her occupation, offered to install a central-heating plant. But she would have none of it—and to this day, as far as I know, Marlborough House remains unheated. She preferred coal fires, of which she had a large number lit, from room to room, by part of the army of some forty servants which she used to employ. Only on an exceptionally cold day would she relent so far as to supplement these with a modest electric radiator, placed beside her chair.

The unheated houses and palaces of my mother's and father's day called for an extra weight of winter clothing. Our suits were always made of an especially thick material. Today however I possess no such thing as a 'winter suit'. My clothes are made from the same weight of material, winter and summer alike.

And so it is throughout America. The heat of American apartments and offices does inevitably breed more casual habits of costume than ours. The waistcoat, gradually dying, as I have already remarked, in Britain, is almost dead in the United States. There, moreover, it is a common practice, unless in the company of visitors, to take off your jacket on entering a room or an office. Business executives do not, it is true, usually go so far as to remove their ties as well, as I am inclined to do myself. But they tend to loosen them at the neck and to unbutton their collars, tightening and fastening them again when a client is announced. On his arrival they will probably invite him to remove his coat. This habit does not yet seem to prevail in Britain, where rooms, though heated, are still kept at a more moderate temperature. Last year in the heat of an exceptional summer in London, I had a conference, in my hotel suite, with three businessmen. They were surprised, I think, to find me awaiting them in my shirt-sleeves, but still more surprised, and equally pleased, when I invited them to follow my example and remove their coats. They did so with smiles of relief, and our conference proceeded in an atmosphere which was cooler and more relaxed.

But it is in his tropical-weight clothes that the American male 'goes to town', as it were. His 'palm beach suits' are made for him in a variety of material and colours. I myself like especially the 'seersucker suit', made of a light ribbed cotton material in stripes of brown, blue or grey. But there are men, especially in Florida and California who, in their light-weight clothes, like to break out into sky blues and other vivid colours. Such flamboyant tastes are, I believe, a produce of the cosmopolitan nature of the American people. Latins and other Southern Europeans tend to dress more gaily than we Anglo-Saxons. America is full of such immigrant stock, American citizens of Italian, Greek, Spanish or Mexican origin, and they have made their imprint on masculine fashions.

But it is in beach clothes, and other kinds of sports clothes, that the Americans are most at ease—and most inventive. In Florida I often have trousers, and indeed jackets, made of a tropical-weight corduroy, in a variety of light colours. Nor do I inhibit myself in the choice of the colours of the open-necked shirts which I wear with them.

But I remain in most ways conservative. When an American woman of my acquaintance kindly offered to give me a waistcoat, embroidered in gros-point and decorated with images of fish or birds or golf-clubs, according to my favourite sport, I politely refused, explaining that I never wear a waistcoat. Instead, I asked her for an embroidered cummerbund, with my monogram on it. And this I often wear in the evenings, down at the Mill.

Elsewhere the clothes of the early American settlers

have made their mark on modern fashions. The lumber-jackets they wore, brightly-coloured so as to stand out from a distance through the forest, have fathered the golfing-jackets and red caps, as a danger signal to discourage the stray shots of less experienced sportsmen.

American working-men's clothes are commendably practical. For all heavy work they wear gloves of an especially thick leather. A few years ago I brought back some pairs of these working gloves, and gave them to my gardeners at the Mill, suggesting that they would effectively protect their hands against briars and splinters. They accepted them politely, but at first, conservative in their instincts, were reluctant to wear them. The other day, however, my Polish gardener came to me with a pair of these gloves, which he had worn out, and begged me to bring him back a new pair from the United States.

When all is said and done, it is perhaps the American cowboys, with their tight-fitting pants, who have had the most widespread influence on masculine costume. In the form of blue jeans these are worn today by the youth of both sexes half the world over and by some with less youthful figures. They are not, I must confess, the pants for me.

CHAPTER XI

SPORTS CLOTHES

In our time, it is primarily sports clothes that have broken away from the previous traditions of male attire. They above all mark the democratic century, with its swing towards freedom and ease. The change in this direction has been strikingly rapid. It is true that, when I myself first came upon the scene, top hats were no longer being worn for cricket. But tennis was still being played in buckskin shoes, tight flannel trousers and stiff collars and ties—usually club ties, fastened with golden safety-pins; and sometimes it was played in white knickerbockers of the type then universally worn for bicycling.

A stiff collar too, with Norfolk jacket and tweed cap, were the regulation uniform for golf—unless indeed you belonged to a club which had its own loose jacket or blazer, in scarlet—as at St. Andrews—or otherwise. For boating, of course, gentlemen wore the straw boater. In my childhood, as I have already recorded, we never wore anything so indelicate as shorts, but only knickerbockers with long stockings for all forms of sport, football included.

It was perhaps in subconscious protest against this that from my earliest period of emancipation I took to sports clothes with especial alacrity. The favourite sport of my youth was hunting, and here indeed I did not find much scope for originality of costume. For the hunting field, as befits its ancient English traditions, remains strict in its conventions as to what a gentleman should wear, and my riding boots with 'mahogany tops' were not so very different from those of my Georgian forbears. Moreover my hunting-coat was very similar in cut to the coat that a gentleman wore in the street in the early nineteenth century.

I was however bold enough to introduce one innovation: a new form of knitted sleeveless sweater to take the place of the thick buttoned waistcoat which I never found comfortable for hunting. I had it made in yellow to wear with a pink coat, and grey to wear with a black one. I first wore it with the Quorn, and it soon had many grateful imitators.

Later my favourite sport became golf, and here I found more scope for indulging my freedom of taste in dress. There was nothing new about plus-fours, though I was given the credit for making them popular. They had become the regulation service dress for officers in the Brigade of Guards, and before that both my father and my grandfather had worn a baggy type of knickerbocker, though it was not so wide and did not fall so low. Possibly, however, my own fell a fraction lower than plus-fours had done hitherto, and it was this that attracted so much attention.

I always had a fondness for tweeds, like my father and grandfather, but I wore mine a trifle more loosely and casually than they. The origin of such materials has always interested me, and in fact tweed, I believe, has nothing to do with the name of the river. Tweeds derive from 'tweels' or twills, the materials produced by a certain process of wool and cotton weaving. The name was misread one day on an invoice, and so became tweeds.

Tweeds first became popular in the nineteenth century, around the time of the Great Exhibition of 1851. Some sensation was created, at this exhibition, by the shepherd's plaid, which quickly became popular for trousers. The credit for the name was appropriated by a manufacturer named Sheppard, who had mills at Frome in Somerset. In fact the real origin of the pattern is much older, dating back to the eighteenth and even the seventeenth century, when it was used, as the name suggests, by shepherds for their plaids in the Lowlands of Scotland.

It was about a century ago or so I have heard, that a pair of trousers was first made of it. When a Scottish merchant, returning from a trip to England, landed at Glasgow, he noticed a man on the quay wearing black-and-white check trousers. He was much struck by the spectacle, since at that time trousers were made only of the plainest drabs and greys and blacks. Seeing that the material had been bleached, not by sulphur, as was usual, but by a long spell of what the Scots call 'peat reek', he assumed that the wearer had cut it from his grandfather's plaid, or his grandmother's shawl.

The trousers attracted some attention, and not long afterwards, a friend in the clothing trade wrote to him from London, asking for a pattern of a 'coarse woollen black-and-white checked stuff' for trousers, made in Scotland. This was not easy to produce, since the material was only woven into plaids, with border and fringes. But he was able to cut a piece from the seam of his brother's cloak, which he sent to his friend, and so a new fashion in trousers was born.

The Victorians took to it, and it is said of Lord Orford, who disapproved of Queen Victoria's marriage to a German prince, that he celebrated the Prince Consort's death putting on a pair of light shepherd's plaid trousers. First worn by the anonymous Scotsman on the quayside at Glasgow, they were the trousers that I myself was to be wearing a century later at Ascot, the most fashionable function of the London season.

Countless variations were to be played on this shepherd's plaid pattern. Colours were to be introduced into it, overchecks super-imposed upon it. District checks were to be evolved, of which the most famous was—and still is—the Glenurquhart. Lowland in their inspiration, these checks bore little relation to the bolder and more colourful tartans of the Highlands.

New checks were soon evolved by Highland lairds, in which to dress their retainers. One was the Mar, designed by the Duff family for their estate in the forest of Mar. The Prince Consort designed the Balmoral, adapting it from the Royal Stuart tartan in a black-and-grey pattern with a bold red overcheck. Worn by the Royal Family, this was also used both to clothe the employees on the estate and to upholster the chairs in the Castle. When I myself became King, I introduced it as the tartan for the pipers at Balmoral, who had hitherto worn the Royal Stuart.

In my grandfather's time a 'Prince of Wales's check'—in red and brown with a blue overcheck—had been introduced for country clothes, and this, wrongly attributed to myself, was to become well known throughout the world, from the nineteen-twenties. Already it had become usual for the regiments of the Brigade of Guards, and others of the Line, to design their own special checks to be worn by their officers for country pursuits.

I have always liked the Highland tartans. In my closets at the Mill I still have a number of old kilts, and I wear this comfortable Highland dress of an evening. They are of the various tartans which I have the right to wear—Royal Stuart, Hunting Stuart, Rothesay, Lord of the Isles, Balmoral. I prefer those which are coloured with the old vegetable rather than the new chemical dyes, since their colours are truer. Several of these I obtained from the late Duchess of Sutherland, who revived and encouraged the old dyeing industry at Dunrobin Castle.

The kilts I wear are shorter than those of my father and grandfather, but not so short as those worn by my forbears in the early nineteenth century—by George IV for example and his brother the Duke of Sussex, as painted by Wilkie. Their length at that time was approved by a true Scotsman, Sir Walter Scott, who stage-managed the King's visit to Edinburgh, soon after his Accession, and put even the Lowland gentry into kilts, to the delight of the clothiers, who designed over a hundred new tartans for the royal visit. The Prince Consort, however, certainly no Scotsman but an enthusiastic admirer of all things Scottish, introduced what might be called the 'German kilt', so decently long as almost to cover the knees, and it was this length that prevailed at Court right down to my father's time.

Sporrans had by then grown longer too, with the gradual substitution of the goat-hair or horse-hair sporran for the smaller pouch which prevailed until the end of the eighteenth century. By Victorian times these hairy appendages were hanging well below the apron of the kilt. I never cared for them myself, preferring the earlier and neater design.

My father's tartan suit, which I also wear in the evenings at the Mill, began to influence fashions, curiously enough, half a century after it was made in the eighteen-nineties. I happened to wear it one evening for dinner at La Croe near Antibes, where the Duchess and I lived for a while after the last war. One of our guests mentioned the fact to a friend in the men's fashion trade, who immediately cabled the news to America. Within a few months tartan had become a popular material for every sort of masculine garment, from dinner jackets and cummerbunds to swimming-trunks and beach shorts. Later the craze even extended to luggage.

Under the influence of the Highlands, I used to enjoy playing the bagpipes, an instrument upon which, however, I never became very proficient. I would practise on the 'chanter' whenever I had a free moment. Once, when I was doing so in my sleeper on the Scots Express, *en route* for Balmoral, one of the attendants, surprised by this wailing sound, remarked to my detective: 'What's he got in there? A bag of snakes?'

I took my bagpipes wherever I went, even when travelling abroad. Once, while on a yachting trip, I even composed a tune. I took my pipes ashore when we anchored off a lonely spot on the coast of Mallorca. Inspired no doubt by these romantic surroundings, I found myself breaking into an air of my own invention. I was able to keep the melody in my head until my return home, when I had it set to music by my father's old Pipe-Major, Henry Forsyth, who had originally taught me to play the instrument. Under the title of 'Mallorca' it has since been played as a slow march by the pipers of the Scots Guards.

My taste for tweeds was matched by a taste for woollens—for sweaters of all kinds, for bright-patterned stockings. I suppose the most showy of all my garments was the multicoloured Fair Isle sweater, with its jigsaw of patterns, which I wore for the first time while playing myself in as Captain of the Royal and Ancient Golf Club at St. Andrews in 1922. Its consequent widespread popularity brought some relief, I like to think, to many a Hebridean crofter family.

My sweater was, I fear, the only outstanding feature of my appearance at St. Andrews on that occasion. To nerve myself for the inaugural drive, I did a thing I have never done before or since. I downed a dram of whisky before my breakfast. It was not alas effective! Before the early morning crowds, with a bunch of caddies lined up a decent way down the course in the hope of retrieving my ball and so earning a golden sovereign, I made so bad a tee shot, when the traditional cannon was fired, that I had the humiliation of seeing them all run a long way towards me before the first of them reached the ball.

On my medal round later that morning I played a little better. To my father I wrote: 'I think I didn't play too bad golf, though my "stunt drive" at 8.30 a.m. Wednesday wasn't a very good one.' I trust he did not see the banner headline in a local Scots newspaper: 'What the Prince said when he topped his drive.'

When my brother, the Duke of York, was in turn elected Captain and had to undergo the same ordeal a few years later, he determined to improve upon this bad tee-shot of mine. We used to play golf regularly together. But during the few months before his approaching ordeal I noticed that he made excuses not to play with me. Only later did I discover that he was devoting his leisure to practising assiduously with his driver. His patience was rewarded when he played himself in at St. Andrews with a magnificent tee-shot, which sent the ball soaring far over the heads of the assembled caddies.

In a few years—whenever the British climate allowed—I was shedding jacket, sweater and tie to play golf in my shirt-sleeves, a practice which had horrified an earlier generation of Scots golfers. Shirt-sleeves, the *Tailor and Cutter* had pronounced in 1913, were 'against the etiquette of the game'. Now they were to become a normal costume for golfers, in warm weather at any rate. The Argentinians, after my visit, were all playing golf in open-necked, short-sleeved shirts and light flannel plus-fours, as I had done.

Soon I was playing it not merely bare-armed and bare-necked but bare-headed as well. At first I discarded the tweed cap for the handier beret. Then I discarded that too, preferring to play hatless. Only in America, as a protection against glare, do I sometimes wear one of those linen golf caps with a peak, of which I have a large collection.

I never had any great fondness for hats, and it was odd the other day to come upon an old letter to me from the late Lord Esher, a favourite in Court circles in my grandfather's time, which he wrote in 1921: 'I want a photo of you *without* a hat, if there is such a thing.' Today it would be hard to find a photograph of me *with* a hat. As a concession to convention however I usually wear a hat while walking in a city.

The other day, when the Duchess and I were invited to a wedding in New York, I found I had no bowler to wear. So I went into a shop and bought one. It was a new kind of bowler, made of a soft, light felt—in fact a soft hat disguised as a hard one. After buying this hat, I noticed a curious thing. Walking in a soft hat down Park Avenue towards the shop, I had been recognized by no one. But when I came out of it and walked up the street again, wearing the bowler, people at once turned round to look at me and saw who I was. To such an extent does the bowler hat—to say nothing of the 'stuffed shirt'—attract attention in New York as an integral part of the Britisher's make-up.

I never wore a brown or a grey bowler, as my father used to do. But I did try during the 'twenties to launch a dark blue one. It did not catch on. Nor alas did the straw boater which, with the fortunes of the Luton straw hat industry in mind, I made determined efforts to revive during the depression of the 'thirties. A rhymed advertisement of the period read:

BOATERS AHOY!

Two 'boaters' afloat in Leicester Square,
God bless the Prince of Wales.
Now you bright young things who always swear,
Whatever the task entails

To follow his lead—your duty indeed
Is clear-cut and simple. 'Tis that
No matter what urgent claims others may plead
You purchase a new boater hat.

But even such flights of poetry did not inspire many 'bright young things' to do so, and the fashion died a second, and doubtless final, death.

During the last three decades, it is maybe beach clothes that have been responsible for the most striking development in men's attire. From the nineteen-twenties onwards it was no longer considered indelicate to expose bare limbs to the sunlight. Sun-bathing grew popular and, for the first time in its history, the South of France became a favourite resort for a summer rather than a winter holiday. Britons flung off their conventional clothes and started to dress like Mediterranean fishermen, in singlets and heavy linen trousers of various colours. I myself began to enjoy, on my annual vacation in search of the sun, 'going native' in this relaxed and easy fashion. I liked to lie out for hours in the sun, toasting my skin to a rich brown tan, and thus, I thought, storing up heat rays inside me against the cold of the British winter to come.

When, as King, I went for a cruise down the Adriatic and around the Eastern Mediterranean in the *Nahlin*, with a party of friends, which included my wife-to-be, my informal costume meant that I was not always recognized by the crowds when we landed. Lady Diana Cooper, who was with us, remembers me walking among the villagers on a Dalmatian island, hatless, in a pair of shorts, a blue-and-white striped shirt, and rope-soled shoes. 'Half of them,' she writes in her memoirs, 'didn't know which the King was and must have been surprised when they were told.'

On all my travels at home and abroad—I was for many years accompanied by a shrewd and stalwart Scotsman named David Storier, my police officer. Storier had succeeded Police Inspector Burt, a man of such infinite resource that he became known to the Press as my 'walking wardrobe'. He had two inner pockets in his coats as capacious as those of a gamekeeper, from which he could produce on request any object I might require, from an apple to an aspirin—to say nothing of a wide selection of articles of clothing.

Storier, when he took his place, did not conceive it as part of his duties to serve me as a kind of human emporium. One of my staff, accustomed to Burt, was once piqued at receiving a negative answer from Storier in reply to a request for a safety-pin. 'What, no safety-pin?' he exclaimed in irritation, as though this were a normal item in every police officer's equipment.

But Storier was in other ways equally versatile. He used to describe himself as my Acting-A.D.C., Secretary, Valet, Fool and, incidentally, Police Officer-in-Attendance. When, as sometimes happened, I travelled without Crisp, my valet, Storier would bring me my morning tea and valet me like an expert. Being himself a remarkably well-dressed man, this self-imposed task came to him naturally enough.

When we were in Scotland, he would find for me in the shops those red and white spotted handkerchiefs, made of cotton, in which the British workman, before the days of the Welfare State, used to carry his lunch, and which were now becoming increasingly hard to find in England.

I liked to use these handkerchiefs for the purpose, not of carrying my lunch, but of blowing my nose, since I found that the cotton of which they were made was both strong and, when washed, remarkably soft.

It was the resourceful Storier who accompanied me to Austria after my Abdication. After our arrival at the castle of Enasfeld, where I was to stay with Baron Eugene de Rothschild, I felt the need, after my journey, for a Turkish bath, a form of civilized relaxation to which I had grown accustomed in London. I had developed the habit of going to the Hammam Baths in Jermyn Street—destroyed, alas, in the war—and of taking a steam bath there, followed by a massage from a stalwart and much-tattooed ex-sailor. Here Crisp would be awaiting me, with my clothes for the day laid out in a cubicle, and I would face my duties refreshed in body and mind.

Crisp, in places where there was no 'Hammam', had learned to rig me up a makeshift steam bath. But now he was no longer with me, and the Rothschilds' valet did not know how this was done. But Storier knew, and immediately got an electric kettle boiling, placed it under a chair, seated me upon it, and wrapped me up in towels until I was soon perspiring happily.

Jack Crisp kept a notebook in which, over the years, he jotted down my various requirements. Under the heading 'Biarritz 1933' I find the note: 'Take next time mosquito net. Torch and batteries. Kettle and Meta or Electric Kettle. Spray and scent. Sheets and pillow cases and towels,' together with 'Bathing Costumes, Panama Hats, Sun Glasses, all coloured Beach Shoes'.

These notes illustrate some of the trials of a royal valet so trained in protocol as to forget no single detail of dress or decorations. Under the heading of 'Freemasons, Edinburgh', I read, following a full inventory of my Highland regalia, 'Take bonnet next time.' For a dinner at Buckingham Palace on the occasion of the funeral of my aunt, Princess Victoria: 'Trousers, stiff shirt, white tie. Black front stud. Black waistcoat. Danish star top Norwegian under. No ribbons, medals.' For Derby Day: 'Field-glasses and pencil. Buttonhole.' For the opening of Parliament: 'Did not wear Victoria Chain, ought to next time.' Under Trooping the Colour, on the other hand: 'No Victorian Chain.'

Only once did Crisp make a mistake. I had travelled up to Ayr on the night train from London to visit and inspect the Royal Scots Fusiliers. When I came to change into uniform I found that I had the wrong khaki service dress tunic. The officer commanding the depot however, immediately came to my rescue. He summoned off the parade ground a young ensign of about my size and ordered him to take off his tunic. My medals were immediately attached to the tunic and I appeared on parade correctly dressed as Colonel-in-Chief. The young officer only learnt afterwards that his tunic had been worn that day by the Prince of Wales.

On holiday in Mallorca. It was on this occasion that I composed the piece of pipe music, 'Mallorca'

Riding back from a rehearsal for the King's Birthday Parade

As King, riding to the Trooping the Colour, 1936

June, 1937; with Wallis and me in this wedding picture taken at the Château Candé, is my best man, Major 'Fruity' Metcalfe

Wallis and I as guests of George Macdonald on a visit to Miami

At the memorial service for Major Metcalfe, talking with Lady Alexandra Metcalfe, his widow

Shooting in Alsace in 1951, wearing my short stalking trousers in Balmoral tartan. Wallis was an interested spectator

In our country home near Paris, I use a ceremonial bass drum of the Welsh Guards as a casual table

CHAPTER XII

FOR THE OCCASION

The Mill is our country home, where we spend week-ends and holidays throughout the year. Although it is only twenty-two miles from Paris, the countryside in which it is situated is tranquil and remote—so remote that our guests are led to the Mill by a map which I drew and have had reproduced, lest our invitations for a quiet week-end be misconstrued as challenges to go exploring the back roads of the valley of the Chevreuse.

The table on which, as King Edward VIII, I signed the instrument of Abdication, now stands in the corner of a room at our Mill. It is a Chippendale table, and on it today is a brass plate recording this historic event, together with the time and date '10.30 a.m. December 10, 1936'. The room is a spacious one, a barn once used by the miller for storing grain, and the Duchess and I call it our Museum.

It contains a number of relics and souvenirs of that life of mine, as Prince of Wales and as King, which I have tried to reflect in these passages. On the book-cases stand some illuminated addresses of welcome presented to me on various civic occasions around the world. Above them hang three documents of which I am especially proud—my Commission in the Royal Navy signed by my father, Sir Winston Churchill as First Lord of the Admiralty, and my relative Prince Louis of Battenberg, as First Sea Lord; my commission in the Army, also signed by my father, and a Mention in Despatches by Sir Douglas Haig, signed again by Winston Churchill, as Secretary of State for War.

On the walls hang pipe banners of the Seaforth Highlanders. On the floor lie big drums of the Grenadier and Welsh Guards, which we now use as occasional tables. Distributed around the room are such objects as steeple-chasing and pig-sticking trophies, a frame containing a specimen of every button in the British Army during the First World War—many from regiments that have since been disbanded—*kukris* given to me by the Gurkhas in India, a bronze statuette of a hunter from Fruity Metcalfe, and three golf balls mounted in silver to commemorate the three accidental occasions on which I made a hole-in-one—at Santos, Brazil, Royal Wimbledon and Nassau, Bahamas.

This is a cheerful room of ours, and its atmosphere is inevitably more intimate than the rooms of Windsor Castle, where I spent so restricted a time in my youth. Moreover, it looks out into an intimate garden, spreading away from the french windows, such as Windsor, endowed only with formal lawns and courtyards, lacks.

When we bought the Mill from the French painter, Etienne Drian, several years ago, we took on a job of reconstruction that literally began with bare walls. The cluster of buildings, some of which went back to the seventeenth century, was overgrown with vines. The vines had to be stripped off, before our remodelling began leaving the walls naked, which measured two feet thick.

The gardens I took as my province, while the Duchess took the interiors as hers, graciously accepting my suggestions for some of the furnishings as I did hers in the landscaping. Since she loves to arrange flowers in vases throughout the house, I converted the kitchen garden into one for cut flowers. The Mill is the first home we have ever owned together, and on it, we have lavished the affection and ideas we stored up during the fifteen years we lived in rented houses in Paris and the Rivieria, in hotels, and in Government House at Nassau during my wartime service as Governor of the Bahama Islands.

Although the Mill has been transformed—its barn into our Museum, a small storeroom adjoining the barn into our outdoor dining-room, its stables into small bedrooms for our bachelor guests, bathrooms and central heating installed where there was none—the work is not yet completed, and if I am any authority in these matters, never will be. We are presently putting in a swimming-pool, which, I hope, will give us and our guests as much pleasure in warm weather as did the one at Fort Belvedere, where the Duchess and I, and our companions of that time, spent the few carefree days we were able to enjoy in the tense summer preceding the Abdication. As I have written elsewhere, I am a genuine 'dirt gardener', working alongside the three gardeners in my employ, and not a mere dilettante observing them at work. Ours is a garden with herbaceous borders, and across a tumbling river fringed with willows, we have built a rock garden which loses itself up a wooded hill. Here I like to work, planting, weeding, and pruning in old clothes and rubber boots, and to play with our pug dogs, named respectively: Disraeli, Trooper, Davy Crockett, and the Imp. The pug is a breed which was first introduced into Britain by William III, and of which my grandmother, Queen Alexandra, was fond among many others. Queen Victoria, on the other hand, preferred Pekingese, which first came to Britain as survivors of the destruction of the Summer Palace in Peking in the eighteen-sixties, and Pomeranians, of which a larger breed were originally German sheep-dogs. My mother never cared for dogs at all, and while my father had gun dogs, he really liked his parrot best. But the Duchess and I love our pugs, who are affectionate if sometimes unruly companions. They travel with us wherever we go—except alas to Britain.

Browsing around this Mill and garden of ours, I look back half a century, and reflect once more on the many changes through which I have lived. Today, life is far more informal than it was, and this is something on the credit side. People no longer stand on so much ceremony, in their relations with one another. In my father's day the stiffness of behaviour that prevailed at Court was reflected throughout society as a whole. There was not only a rigid conventionality of costume, but an accepted language of polite greetings and phrases which tended to make conversation a stilted and artificial affair. Such conventions still tend to prevail in France, but no longer in Britain or in America. Here manners have become easier—maybe sometimes too much so.

The French, I find, are often shocked by the casual

demeanour of the British, and there may indeed be a tendency on our part to go to the opposite extreme from our ancestors, in the off-handedness of our greetings and the frankness of our conversational exchanges. This is an informal age, compared to that of my youth. But informality is in no sense incompatible with the politeness and consideration which good manners imply. It is possible to be both relaxed and dignified, friendly and reserved, to achieve an easy intimacy and yet to preserve the outward forms of politeness. Without them society is a graceless affair—as some of the younger generation have yet to realize. I have always made it a personal practice never to take anything for granted and never to let a service done go without a thank you.

I have also noticed in this, the hey-day of the psychiatrist, a tendency in some quarters to regard good manners as a mark of personal insecurity. My experience has been quite the contrary. Some of my American friends with many small grandchildren have urged me to write an essay on good manners. Maybe some day I will.

For now, may I note that courtesy and manners serve as a lubricating oil which helps keep human relations from becoming unbearable on this ever more densely populated globe. The closer people are thrown together, the more they must respect one another.

Again, life is less static than it used to be. Its rhythm has quickened. People live more energetically, breaking away from routine to engage more freely in every kind of activity. They get around more, meet a greater variety of people, and see more of foreign lands. Air travel of course makes this easier—and this is on the credit side too.

But if people play harder, they also work harder. Few

of my contemporaries, before the First World War, had to earn a living. In that era, there was a class of people—I am speaking of the Britain which I know—who owned landed estates and did not have to work for their support. They had plenty of time for sports and what is usually referred to as the leisurely life. But after the war, everything changed. Men began going to offices in the West End or in the City, every day with only their week-ends free to pursue their favourite sports. Those who had to do so were at first looked upon by their more fortunate friends with a certain degree of compassion. I can recall older people pitying poor So-and-so because he had to go into the City to work, and couldn't hunt for six days a week any more. All he had now was a week-end. Indeed, that was only the beginning of the changes these older people saw. Now almost all of them work in some capacity or another, and this is the accepted order of things. (No wonder the top hat and frock-coat are things of the past!)

As a result, all the strata of society co-mingle. Instead of remaining in his own little group, seeing only a few people, talking only about the things that interest those few people, everyone moves about more. These are changes that I endorse, and which are reflected, in some degree, by my own life.

The Duchess, who likes a man to 'dress up', is inclined to be critical of the fact that nowadays he tends rather to 'dress down'. Whether in New York or in London, a man seldom puts on evening dress if he is going to a restaurant or a theatre. The Duchess argues that, if women dress up for an evening out, as we like them to do, men should pay them the compliment of doing the same.

On the other hand, life being as it is today, it is I think unreasonable to expect men to dress up as often as they used to do in a more leisurely age. New York, and to an increasing extent London, are business cities, where men work in offices from morning until evening. Most New Yorkers have to travel long distances each day, by train or motor-car, from homes in the country and back there at night. They have no time or place in which to change for the evening, as they would at home. Londoners, on the other hand, live more often in London itself, and so have less excuse not to do so.

I like to dress for dinner, especially when we are dining with friends in their homes. But when I go out to a restaurant, on the principle of 'doing in Rome as the Romans do', I find myself, all too often, wearing day clothes in the evening. In our own home I always dress for dinner, even if it is only in a velvet cord dinner-jacket. And I like our guests to do the same.

When it comes to day clothes, for wear in town, these must now be essentially practical, with few of those refinements of style in which the leisured dandies of the past could indulge. Beau Brummell, we must remember, never had to travel in a bus. Nor, for that matter, as Sir Derek Keppel implied in his retort, already quoted, did my father. Today business suits must be dark, so as not to show the dirt; collars must have just enough starch in them not to crease before the end of the day; ties must be discreet, so as to inspire confidence in clients. Town clothes must be reasonably comfortable, to meet the demands of modern life. Yet their tendency is to conform to a more or less uniform style.

It is perhaps for this very reason that country clothes,

with the exception of those worn for the more traditional sports of hunting, shooting and fishing, have become livelier in colour and more casual in style. Obliged to restrain themselves in town, men like to let themselves go in the country. But this laudable aspiration is unlikely, I feel, to be carried too far. Britons have always been noted for a spirit of moderation and compromise. They are fond of understatement, not merely in their words but in their clothes. Today, the well-dressed man combines, in his costume, the practical demands of a workaday life with the elegance required of a man of good taste.

In terms of fashion, London has always been the capital for the man, just as Paris is for the woman. Long may they both remain so!

ACKNOWLEDGEMENTS

I wish to express my appreciation to those who have given me of their time and valuable information in the writing of this book.

Personal:

Mr. James Laver, for reading and checking the accuracy of the MS.

Lady Alexandra Metcalfe; Colonel Sir John Aird; Mr. Robert Mackworth-Young, Librarian at Windsor Castle; Captain W. A. Fellowes, Agent at Sandringham; Mr. John H. Scholes, Curator of Historical Relics, British Transport Museum; Lord Montagu of Beaulieu and the Montagu Motor Museum; Mr. Jack Murdocke, Mr. Charles Graves, Mr. Jack Crisp, Mrs. Charlotte Bill, Mr. Sanford, of Messrs. Hawes and Curtis; Mr. Willington, late of Messrs. Scholte, for providing items of information and refreshing my memory of events.

Mrs. Joan St. George Saunders, of Writer's and Speaker's Research for valuable research work.

Miss Diana de Zouche for typing the MS.

Finally, I wish to acknowledge my debt to Lord Kinross, who has worked with me from the inception of this book.

Published sources:

Useful background information was obtained from the following works:

Windsor Castle by Sir Owen Morshead.

The Windsor Uniform by Sir Owen Morshead. Article in the *Connoisseur,* 1935.

Clothes, and Taste and Fashion by James Laver.

The Works of Max Beerbohm.

Beau Brummell by Kathleen Campbell.

English Dress by Dion Clayton Calthrop.

The History of Underclothes by C. Willett and Phillis Cunnington.

Clothes and the Man by Sydney D. Barney.

The Prince Consort by Roger Fulford.

The Delightful Profession: Edward VII: A Study in Kingship by H. E. Wortham.

The Private Life of King Edward VII by one of His Majesty's Servants.

King Edward VII as a Sportsman by Alfred E. T. Watson.

King George V as a Sportsman by J. Wentworth Day.

Memoirs by Prince von Bülow.

INDEX